Other Titles by Keith R. Rees

Quill and Ink - POETRY

Legend Upon the Cane

By
Keith R. Rees

ISBN 978-0-6152-1181-7

For my mother, Claudia Williams Rees, who was born and raised in Natchitoches, Louisiana.

Prologue

In the mid 17th century, many Indian tribes lived in the areas of eastern Texas and northern Louisiana along the Red River and Sabine River. One such tribe, called the Caddo Indians, lived there long before the first French and Spanish explorers arrived. As time passed, the tribe eventually split into smaller tribes and settled in other nearby areas as explorers began to encroach upon their territory.

At the turn of the 18th century, exploration of the New World was well underway. France and Spain continued to push further into the heart of North America, by way of the Mississippi River. Merely a few decades had passed since the 30 Years' War in Europe, yet tensions still ran high between France and Spain in the New World. The French explorers sought to establish trade with the natives and help them improve their way of life. The Spanish made their way with missionaries that came along to spread the Christian Word to the natives. The race was on, to claim new territory, and establish strategic positions in this part of the New World burgeoning with promise and opportunity. Many times their paths crossed in these strange new lands.

Yet, the explorers were accompanied by only small military fronts. They found it best to travel up the local rivers and tributaries with traders and small companies of soldiers to try and establish good relations with the local Indian tribes. Good progress was made, but resentment and opposition from some tribes was culminating, for the newcomer's presence was not welcome.

French explorers were deeply interested in establishing roots in the fertile lands of the lower Mississippi for purposes of trade and settlement. But, they were also wary of Spanish explorers in Texas pushing into their territory from the West.

For the most part, the native tribes welcomed the newcomers for their livestock trade, and building and farming skills. In turn, the natives showed the settlers the art of hunting in these foreign lands. The land was called *La Louisiane*, or "Land of Louis". Just a few short years earlier, Robert Cavelier de La Salle had claimed the land for France in the name of King Louis XIV. The land would become known as the Louisiana Purchase nearly a century later.

This is a fictional account based on true persons and events in the oldest settlement of this territory, which is nearly three hundred miles inland from the mouth of the Mississippi River. This particular area, near the head of the Red River, was called Natchitoches. It was named for the local tribe, which the French settlers befriended in the early 1700's. The French were led by Louis Juchereau de St. Denis. The story tells of the tribe's settlement in the area, their first encounter in 1701 with the French explorers, their move to Lake Pontchartrain near New Orleans in 1702, and then their eventual, yet historic, return to their homeland in 1714. Their return to a small tributary near the head of the Red River, called the *Riviere aux Cannes*, or the Cane River.

Chapter 1

The light of the fire flickered in the dimming light of a summer sunset. The early evening sounds of marsh crickets and tree frogs echoed through the river valley. A lone Indian brave danced by the light of the fire, dressed in a ceremonial headdress. He chanted low and slowly and stepped lightly on his bare feet. He shuffled through the sand to the sound of a solo drumbeat. He danced to the coming twilight and for the beckoning moon. His chant would rise and fall with the embers that crackled from the fire as he lifted his eyes to the heavens as the smoke rose to bless the air of the coming night.

In a small, mud thatched hut, the glow of a fire could be seen. A new mother's cry sang out into the night, blending with the chant of the spirit guide. Inside the hut, a young squaw gritted her teeth and wailed in pain. Her eyes glistened in the light of the fire, as tears filled her eyes. Aiyana breathed short and quick and she grasped the hand of her caretaker, Onacona, or White Owl. Aiyana threw her head from side to side, crying out in pain. But she kept her eyes fixed on the old woman, knowing that she was in good hands.

As the sun set its last light over the horizon, Aiyana cried out once more. Her breathing became a series of long sighs of relief. Then another faint cry was heard from within the tiny hut. It was the cry of her newborn son. He cried out as he felt the cool night air for the first time. The little one was wrapped in warm, soft fox pelts and was placed in his mothers exhausted arms. Aiyana smiled at her baby, with tears of joy running down her cheeks. The little baby rested in her arms, with his tiny blue eyes opened just slightly. He had a small, damp mat of light colored hair. His eyes closed in the comfort of his mother's arms.

The old woman pulled the door flap aside to reveal an anxious father waiting outside. Chief Caddo stepped into the hut slowly, looking at his young wife and their newborn son.

"Your eyes are shining brightly this night, my wife," he said softly to her.

"Here is our son," Aiyana said in a weak voice.

He placed his hand on the side of her face. She closed her eyes and rested her head against his broad hand. Suddenly, her eyes flew open wide and she wailed in tremendous pain. White Owl came rushing back and took the newborn baby from her arms and placed him in a small bed of fresh grasses and pelts. She quickly looked Aiyana over and instinctively knew what was wrong.

"You must leave now," she said firmly to Caddo.

"Why, what has happened?" he asked frantically.

"There is still another! I must attend to her now!" White Owl exclaimed, pushing him out of the hut. Aiyana's pain was even more severe. She could barely breathe as the pain shot through her body. She gasped for air and held the old woman's hand tightly. White Owl wiped the sweat from Aiyana's face and tried to calm her.

"Easy, my child, easy," she said calmly. "I will stay with you. I will not leave your side."

The ordeal for Aiyana continued into the night and her labor pains intensified with each passing hour. Caddo remained outside in the damp light rain the entire night. White Owl waited patiently at her side, trying to comfort Aiyana and attend to her needs. She kept the fire alit and fresh water at her bedside.

At first light, a light fog covered the Sabine River valley. The rain clouds had dissipated as the faintest of light could be seen over the eastern horizon. The cries of Aiyana could be heard throughout the tribal village. Caddo stared at the ground helplessly. He worried greatly about his wife and wanted her pain to cease.

He gazed into the distance as the morning sun warmed his face. Then, he noticed that he no longer heard the cries of his laboring wife. Suddenly, he heard a low, faint cry coming from the hut. He closed his eyes in relief. She had finally delivered her second baby.

White Owl emerged from the hut, carrying an empty water skin and wearily walked towards the river to refill it.

Caddo grabbed her arm and she looked at him with tired eyes. "She is alright?" he asked her. She nodded and motioned for him to go inside.

Caddo ducked inside the hut slowly to see his thoroughly exhausted wife asleep on the bed. In her arms was another tiny baby, with dark brown eyes, who appeared to be wide awake. He cooed softly, with light, faint cries. His head was covered with thick dark hair that matched the color of his father's. Caddo knelt beside her. He brushed her hair away from her forehead.

"My lovely Aiyana. How brave you are," he said in a whisper. She opened her eyes slowly to see him and then closed them again. "Rest now, my wife. I will not leave your side."

On the third day, the entire Caddo tribe came together on the banks of the river to welcome the newborn babies into their midst. It was tradition to name the newborn on this day and welcome them into the tribe with ceremonial dancing. A great feast was prepared and a large sacred fire was burning in the center of the village.

Aiyana sat with her husband, holding her two newborn sons. Caddo stood before the crowd and all became quiet.

"The 'great spirit' has come upon our village and blessed us with the arrival of not one, but two sons," he said, standing with a firm expression. "We welcome them to our family with

10

dancing amid the sacred smoke that will lift their names to the realm of the 'great spirit'. Let the names of my sons now be spoken!"

Caddo reached down and Aiyana handed him the first of their two sons. He held him in his arms and spoke, "My son, since you came into this world as the sun set over our lands, I shallcall you Nakahodot."

He gave Nakahodot back to Aiyana and then she handed him their second son. He held him close in his arms and spoke, "My son, since you came into this world as the sun rose over our lands, I shall call you Natchitos."

Caddo sat next to his wife and the dancing and singing began. He smiled at his wife and their twin sons. The little ones watched the celebration with wide and fascinated eyes.

As the years passed, Nakahodot and Natchitos grew to be excellent young braves. Their father took pride in teaching them the ways of the Caddo. He taught them to hunt and to fish. Both became very skilled with the spear and the bow and arrow. They learned to work in the fields and plant corn, beans and tobacco. They learned how to use the native trees to construct their homes and build canoes. They learned to fashion mud to the walls of their homes. Caddo took pride in teaching both of his sons the true ways of a young warrior.

Natchitos grew very fond of the river valley where they lived. He loved to explore in the forests by the river. He found a small hill that overlooked their village that provided a view of the river. As he grew older, he would hike up the hill early each morning to watch the sunrise. Aiyana would see him sitting on the hillside staring out over the horizon each morning. She would shake her head and smile and think that her second son was indeed aptly named.

In the fifteenth year of their lives, both young braves were given their father's permission to seek wives to marry. The tribe was close-knit, with a small collection of families that lived amongst one another. So, they both already knew the young squaws with whom they held favor.

Nakahodot came to the hut of Atohi, father of Calanele. He sat with him at the fire and asked him for his daughter's hand in marriage. If Atohi should grant his permission, on the third morning Nakahodot would find blessings outside his door.

Natchitos did the same as his brother. He went to the hut of Nashoba, or Running Wolf, father of Taima. He asked Running Wolf for his daughter's hand in marriage. If Running Wolf should grant his permission, on the third morning Natchitos would find blessings outside his door.

On the third morning, Nakahodot and Natchitos rushed outside their home. Blessings from both families had been placed outside their door, signifying their acceptance from both families.

On the day that both sons were to marry their betrothed, a great gathering was held in front of the sacred fire as the sun rose to the top of the sky. The two brothers stood together in front of their father, and chief of the tribe, Caddo. Nakahodot stood with long, flowing, dusty-brown hair. Natchitos stood with his long flowing black hair. The women of the tribe chanted and danced as they escorted the two young squaws to their wedding. Both of them were dressed in light gray skins that fell to their feet. They wore decorative moccasins that were only worn on such special occasions. They wore colorful beads, woven onto their clothes, and in their hair that was braided long and black. Nakahodot and Natchitos watched curiously as the women proceeded through the village, singing and chanting. A slow, ceremonial drumbeat was heard throughout the village as they walked.

The families of the women stood behind each of them. Each woman stood before her betrothed. The two beautiful young women smiled faintly as they stared at the ground in front of them. As Caddo spoke, Taima raised her head and gave a quick smile to Natchitos, then looked down again when her mother quietly snitched at her.

"The wedding of a father's son is always a joyous day," Caddo began. "For a father to see his two sons at their wedding is beyond words. It pleases me to see this day has come." He looked at his first son. "Nakahodot, Atohi has granted his blessing for you to take his daughter, Calanele, into your home. You will make her your wife and you will honor and protect her all of your days." His son nodded as he stared downward.

Then Caddo looked at Natchitos, "Natchitos, Running Wolf has granted his blessing for you to take his daughter, Taima, into your home. You will make her your wife and you will honor and protect her all of your days." Natchitos looked at his father and nodded.

"This is a special day for me and your mother," Caddo continued. "May this day be remembered by all the Caddo."

A great celebration began that lasted the rest of the afternoon and throughout the night. The wedding of the chief's two sons was a joyous occasion that all of the tribe's people would remember.

Three years had passed when Aiyana fell ill in the coldest days of winter. Caddo stayed by her side night and day as she fought a fever that gripped her entire body. And, on the fourth day of her struggle, Aiyana passed away. Sadness spread among the tribe. Caddo was inconsolable with grief and despair. He could not even gather the strength to carry his wife's body on the solemn procession to lay her to rest, far into the forest. He asked his two sons to carry their mother for him, to take her body to the place where the 'great spirit' would come to take her away.

A period of mourning lasted for three days among the entire tribe.

Chief Caddo was never the same after the passing of his beloved wife. His sons would try to comfort him, but their attempts were futile. As time went on, both brothers started families of their own along the Sabine River. Taima had given birth to her first born, a son, she and Natchitos named Anoki. Natchitos began to teach their son as his father had taught him.

One night, in the middle of summer, word spread throughout the tribe that their chief had grown ill in his old age. Nakahodot and Natchitos rushed to their father's home to be at his side. Caddo gasped for air as he lay on his bed. Natchitos tried to keep a fire lit to help his father stay warm. The two sons sat at his side the rest of the evening and into the night.

As the two men sat in silence with their father, Caddo spoke to them in a weak voice, "My sons, my time has come and soon I will reunite with your mother. My soul has ached for her and now it is time to meet her once again." His two sons listened to him with sadness in their eyes. "The 'great spirit' has provided a fruitful land by the river. But, now it is time for the tribe to find a new land." Nakahodot and Natchitos looked at each other in surprise.

Caddo continued, "Soon, you will both be leaders of the Caddo. My sons, I ask of you this final wish. On the day of my passing, I ask that both of you gather your family and their families and go and settle in new lands. Do not mourn me for three days. Instead, I ask for you to remember me in another way." Both sons listened intently to their father. "Nakahodot, I ask that you travel for three days towards the setting sun. On the third day, you will stop and settle in the new land and rear a tribe."

Then, Caddo looked at Natchitos. "Natchitos, I ask that you travel for three days towards the rising sun. On the third day, you will stop and settle in the new land and rear a tribe.

The 'great spirit' willing, you will both find your way to one another once again, thus continuing the sacred bond of the Caddo. What I ask of you, was done by me, and my father before me. Now, I am asking this of you. This is the only way to ensure the lasting of the Caddo." Both sons sat and thought about what their father had said. They both looked at each other and silently nodded to their father and to one another.

Natchitos looked at his father and said, "We shall honor your request, Father. It will be done." Later that night, Chief Caddo breathed his last.

Both sons did as their father had asked them. With the efficiency of a military garrison, the entire tribe had gathered everything and prepared for the long journey.

Nakahodot gathered his and Calanele's family and other tribal families. They numbered about forty-five in all. Natchitos, in turn, gathered his wife and son, Taima's extended family, and the remaining members of the tribe. In all, they numbered about thirty-five.

The two brothers stood facing one another. They clasped their arms together in the tribe's traditional way.

"Are you certain this is the right thing for us to do? Together, we form a more formidable tribe, do we not?" Nakahodot asked his brother.

"We must honor our father in life and in death," Natchitos responded. "The 'great spirit' will guide us and give us strength. He will guide us to the proper place for mourning. We will know when we have found it. Then, mourning will turn to joy."

Natchitos looked at his brother and said, "I will always think of you, brother. Whenever the sun sets, my thoughts will be with you."

"Go in peace, my brother," Nakahodot said.

With that, both men gathered their tribes and began their journey. Nakahodot traveled west and Natchitos traveled east.

Natchitos traveled through the forests and over the rolling hills on the eastern side of the Sabine River. The trees were tall and many in number. Occasionally, they would find open fields with ample grain. They stopped only to rest and retrieve water from small ponds and streams.

The sun grew hot as they walked on. On the third day, they continued to walk through a thick forest of trees. Soon, they came upon the crest of a hillside. Natchitos stopped to look out over the view. Below the hill was a narrow river that winded calmly towards the south. The river stretched as far as he could see in both directions. They slowly walked down the hill to the banks of the river. Tall, thick stalks of cane grew along the banks.

Natchitos looked at Taima and then at the rest of the tribe. He nodded to himself. *"We have made it, Father. This is the proper place for our tribe,"* he said to himself.

Taima put her arm into his. "We should not walk any longer," she said to him. "This is the place where we should stay and make our home."

"Yes, this is where the 'great spirit' has been leading us," Natchitos agreed.

He turned to the tribe and spoke, "We will wander no further. We will settle our tribe here." From that day forth, the river became known as the 'waters of the cane'.

Chapter 2
1701 - Thirteen Years Later

It was early morning in late summer when the Indian chief made his way up a narrow trail that led to the top of a small cliff. It was the same trail he had walked each morning, rain or shine, for over a decade now. The trail was narrow with tall strands of grass on either side, flowing back and forth in the breeze. The top of the hill was shaded by large trees and a few clouds from overhead.

This day he was weary from two straight months in the fields trying to salvage what they could from the corn and bean fields. They were able to save most of the corn and some of the beans, but the hot sun, with little rain, assured them of no tobacco or even pumpkins in the fall.

He sat cross-legged on the top of the cliff, overlooking the calm river that wandered through his tribe's village. Natchitos faced the rising sun coming over the horizon. He liked to sit and watch as the wind blew softly through the tall trees all around him. He was now a man of about thirty years. He had seen great battles and lived to tell stories about them. His skin was dark and had grown worn from the wind and dry summers. But he was wise beyond his years and knew how to handle the hard times that his tribe had faced. His thoughts were deep, as usual, thinking about many things, but mostly of how his family and fellow tribesman could withstand this land for much longer on so little food. The years had gone by with success in growing fields of corn and beans, but now things had changed in the skies. The weather was becoming too harsh to keep the crops alive. Each summer had grown hotter, and the rains were not coming as often. This weighed heavy on his mind. But also he thought of his brother, and wondered if he and his family were faced with such challenges as well. *"Surely they must,"* he thought.

Natchitos sat calmly, staring out across the land, when a sudden gust of wind came upon him. A dove stirred from its roost and flew past him. The wind calmed and blew softly for only a few moments more. But, he felt as though the wind, or someone, was tapping him on the shoulder. He looked up and the down the river, but saw nothing. It soon stopped and then he fixed his gaze once again out across the land in front of him, occasionally drawing his finger in the dirt around him. Suddenly he heard a call from below in the village. "Father!" was the cry from below, in a sharp, yet hushed voice. Natchitos looked to see Anoki, his oldest son, pointing frantically upriver. Natchitos looked to his left to see two small rafts, carrying five white men each, coming slowly downriver. He immediately remembered encounters with two other white explorers several years earlier. The one he remembered hearing about was called, LaSalle. *"They did not show us harm,"* he thought. *"They only passed through this area, nothing more. But why do they come now again?"* His instincts felt differently, as he watched them slowly near the village. His thoughts were confirmed when he spotted an Indian guide riding along with the white men.

Natchitos made his way down the cliff back into the village. Anoki was now beside himself with fear and anxiety, waving towards Natchitos to come more quickly. Natchitos could see the rest of the tribe was also well aware of the foreigner's presence. He motioned to his wife Taima to take the children inside the hut and made the same gesture to the rest of the tribe looking on.

"Anoki, be calm, it is alright. It is Buffalo Tamer, I know him. He has a good heart. I will go and talk with him," Natchitos said.

But Anoki persisted, "But Father, who are the white men with him? I would not trust them so quickly. There are so many!"

"I will take Tooantuh with me," Natchitos said. At the same moment, Tooantuh was already striding along with him towards the river shore. Tooantuh was Natchitos' closest and most trusted companion. He was known as a fierce and fearless fighter and an excellent hunter. He took pride in providing big game for the tribe. But he had little patience for intruders, not as much as the trusting Natchitos.

The travelers were paddling their rafts towards the west shore, where Natchitos and Tooantuh stood. All the men sat in both rafts, except for one man in the first raft. He stood with one foot upon the bow, with one hand resting on his knee, the other hanging at his side. Tooantuh looked intently for any sign of weapons, but saw none. Their casual approach showed no sense of attack. Yet still, his arrows rested on his back at the ready. Natchitos stood with a wooden staff in his left hand. He could see the man up front plainly now. He observed how he was dressed, long dark trousers with black boots and a dark blue overcoat, with a white ruffled shirt protruding through the top of his coat. He wore a black triangle hat, with the point just to the left of his head. Their appearance seemed very odd to Natchitos and Tooantuh, considering the days hot sun and how many pelts it must have taken to fashion such clothing.

As the raft came to rest in the mud and grass on the riverbank, the standing man stepped down to the ground in front of Natchitos and Tooantuh, a mere ten yards in front of them. Natchitos raised his right hand in front of him, as if to say, *"That's far enough!"*

"Greetings to you, Bride les Boeufs," Natchitos said in his own language. The man did not understand and turned to see Bride les Boeufs, which means Buffalo Tamer, now standing in the raft behind him. It was the Indian guide in the raft along with them.

"Hello my old friend," Buffalo Tamer said. He hopped off the raft and walked straight up to Natchitos with a smile. "I ask for your grace and kindness to welcome these men. We have traveled down from the Yatasi. They have entrusted me as their guide."

"The Yatasi? Smart they are to employ you, my good friend. You are the best tracker I know," Natchitos said. They clasped their right arms together in the traditional greeting. "Why are the whites here? Can you make the white talk?"

Just then, the white man standing behind Buffalo Tamer spoke up. "I am Lieutenant Louis Juchereau de St. Denis. I come in peace in the name of Louis XIV, King of France."

Buffalo Tamer looked back at St. Denis with a scowling expression. It was not yet the time for him to speak to the chief. But he knew that the white leader always seemed to speak out of turn. He shook his head and allowed him to continue.

"I and my companions humbly present ourselves before you and offer our friendship," St. Denis said. Buffalo Tamer translated St. Denis' words to Natchitos.

Natchitos replied, "If your desire is to visit our land in peace, then we accept your presence here." Tooantuh gave Natchitos a frown. He never liked the way Natchitos accepted strangers in their land so easily. "But, I do not know of this France of which you speak. Why have you come here?"

"We have come from the Yatasi tribe, where, with the aid of Buffalo Tamer, we have established an agreement to trade with them," St. Denis continued. "We are hoping to do the same with you. We have goods to trade with you and have different methods of raising crops that we can show you. In return, all we ask is to be able to live upon your land for only a short period of time. We only wish to live in peace alongside you."

Natchitos listened to his words with a perplexed look upon his face. *"Why now?"* he thought to himself. *"And why would the Yatasi make agreements with this man?"* He pulled Buffalo Tamer to the side. "Buffalo Tamer, what do you think of this man? Can he and these other soldiers be trusted?"

"He's a good man," Buffalo Tamer replied. "They have treated me well and have done all the things that they have spoken to among the Yatasi. I believe his heart is a good one. We were only among the Yatasi for two weeks before coming down the Cane."

Natchitos grew silent and thought longer about what Buffalo Tamer was saying. It seemed to him that it would take much longer than just two weeks time to make an agreement with the Yatasi. What was it about this white man that was so trustworthy?

Buffalo Tamer broke the silence. "He is a good man, but he talks too much." Natchitos gave him a coy grin.

The soldiers began to step off the rafts. Tooantuh noticed immediately that the soldiers did indeed have muskets with them. "Chief," he whispered to Natchitos, and motioned towards the soldiers. Natchitos saw the rifles and looked back over at Tooantuh then back at St. Denis sternly.

Among the six soldiers was a sergeant, Henri LaRouche. He casually barked orders at the other men, with a satchel over one shoulder and his rifle dangling from his other hand. "Gather that gear out of those boats! Come on, I don't have all day!" He wiped the sweat off his brow, scanning over the tribal village and the tall trees on both sides of the river. "What the hell are we doing here?" he muttered to himself.

LaRouche never liked the natives. And he detested these excursions up and down the rivers seeking them out and making treaties with them. He longed to be back in the comfortable confines of the fort at St. Jean. *These people are animals,* he thought to himself, *We should be able to take these lands without question. They could never match the might of the French Army.* He stood oft to the side a few paces from St. Denis, trying to hear what were being said between the Lieutenant and the Indians. He stared at them intently. Then he caught Tooantuh's eye.

21

Tooantuh stared right back at him. LaRouche's stare gave him an uncomfortable feeling.

"How did he convince the Yatasi so quickly?" Natchitos asked Buffalo Tamer. "They are not so easily persuaded. I am curious to hear more."

St. Denis interrupted them, "I would like to introduce one of my officers and the governor of the Fort St. Jean. This is Jean-Baptiste Le Moyne de Bienville. He is my trusted friend and leader."

"It is my pleasure to meet you, Sir," Jean-Baptiste said. "I have heard great things about you."

"I am Natchitos, chief of the Nashitosh. Welcome to you and your men. This is Tooantuh. Tonight you will eat with us at the fire."

St. Denis knew this was a great honor and a very good sign. He hoped that a good foundation was already being laid with these people. They went further down the river and set up camp there.

St. Denis was just over twenty-five years of age when he began his exploration of Louisiana. He was born the eleventh of twelve children in Beauport, New France in 1674, in the area which is now known as Quebec, Canada. His parents were able to send him to France to further his education. But in his heart, he was always an explorer. He had heard stories and read some accounts of the early explorers in the southern regions of the New World, and he had always wanted to see them. He returned from France in 1699 and helped settle a fort along the Mississippi River and one on Biloxi Bay. The former was Fort St. Jean, which would become New Orleans in 1716. It is where he first met Jean-Baptiste Le Moyne de Bienville.

Jean-Baptiste was impressed with the young Frenchman and his ability to calmly establish relationships with the natives. In early 1701, he asked St. Denis to go on a mission upriver on the Mississippi where he had heard it was inhabited by many different tribes. The many connecting river routes further north were key in reaching other areas of exploration and establishing trade routes. As governor, he wished to go along on the journey to see this land himself and to make known that the French explorations were not cursory ones. He trusted and respected St. Denis deeply, but he was a man that wanted to know and see things for himself.

"What do you make of this Chief Natchitos, Louis? A quiet fellow isn't he?" Jean-Baptiste asked.

"Yes, quiet indeed," he replied. "But be patient friend. I know he has much more to say. I see wisdom behind those eyes of his. You know what they say about still waters...still waters run deep!"

Jean-Baptiste laughed heartily. "Yes they do, Louis. His friend was even quieter though. Yet he appeared to be quite fierce. I wouldn't want to cross his path," he quipped. St. Denis chuckled to himself. "How do you think it will go this evening? Do you think we should we go back?"

St. Denis looked surprised, "Of course we should! We've been invited. And I have something for our great chief that might impress him. I think it might take more than just supplies and tools to win this one over. I sensed an obvious concern coming forth from both of them. We don't know how many they number, so we mustn't be too casual in our approach."

"But, Buffalo Tamer said they only number no more than fifty," responded Jean-Baptiste.

"Nevertheless, we number less than ten, including some men that are, shall we say, less than enthusiastic to be on this journey," St. Denis said matter-of-factly. "I plan to drive some spirit back into these stubborn men but I feel I must give them leave before doing so. We've been pressing on for many weeks now and with little rest."

The sunset was nearing and camp was setup for the night. St. Denis, Jean-Baptiste and the soldiers set out back upriver to the tribal village with torch lights. As they approached the landing, a warrior in ceremonial headdress, stood along the shore at tension, staring out into the night, never turning to look at the explorers. He stood with a lit torch stuck in the ground holding it out with a firm straight arm.

"What a magnificent sight!" St. Denis thought to himself. *"This will be a night to remember."*

The soldiers pulled the boats ashore and they all stood on the banks near the warrior, who stood motionless with little expression on his face.

"We must wait here," Buffalo Tamer said to St. Denis. "We must wait until the tribe's spirit guide comes to escort us into the village." St. Denis understood well. A few soldiers swatted their arms and necks at the mosquitoes flying all around the riverside.

"Cursed bloodsuckers," Jean-Baptiste swore under his breath as he slapped the back of his neck for the tenth time, "Leave me in peace!" He swatted at his neck once more. "They are just as bothersome as they are down at the fort, eh Louis? They don't seem to bother this fellow at all. I wonder what his secret is." The warrior seemed to be untouched by all the pesky mosquitoes. St. Denis leant an unsympathetic smile to his colleague as he swatted the back of his neck as well.

Then they heard footsteps coming from within the trees. Out into the clear emerged an impressive figure, wearing a large ceremonial headdress, with decorative skins around his waist that covered the length of his legs. On his chest he wore a vest of colored beads situated in an intricate design. St. Denis was astonished to see that the man was Natchitos himself. He stood motionless, staring into the night sky, as did the warrior standing guard by the river. Then finally looking over at St.

24

Denis, he said bluntly, "Come!" They followed him into the trees towards the village. The warrior remained at his post beside the river.

As they walked the path behind the chief, flickers of firelight were visible, and drumbeats and chants could be heard from the tribal area. The spirit guide approached an open area where a large fire was burning in the middle. Surrounding the fire were numbers of grass thatch and mud covered huts. These were the homes of the Nashitosh Indians. All the tribesmen and women were dressed in ceremonial dress, sitting on the ground in small groups as the troupe approached. A small band of three drummers sat at the right side of the fire, playing a welcome drumbeat and chanting in unison. It was the traditional chant given to guests to welcome them to the village.

St. Denis and Jean-Baptiste looked on in amazement. The soldiers stood behind them with wide eyes. What an incredible sight! They watched as the performance continued. Natchitos walked a few steps further to the left side of the fire and stood next to a woman who had two young children beside her, and a young man dressed in a feather headdress, no more than fourteen years of age. It was Anoki, Natchitos' oldest son. The woman was his wife, Taima. It was apparent that she was with child, perhaps six months along. As his feet came to rest beside her, the drumbeat and chant stopped abruptly.

The French looked on speechless. They knew the chief was about to speak, so they waited and watched intently. Natchitos then said, "I am Natchitos, chief! This is my family, and these are my people. We welcome you to our village. Tonight we will dance for you in front of this sacred fire. We dance for rain, and we dance to call the 'great spirit' to give thanks to him. Tonight you will eat with us by the fire." One of the women motioned to the visitors to sit in an open spot next to the chief's family, a sitting place that had been left open just for them. The woman was Tooantuh's wife, Ayita.

25

Ayita was young and beautiful, no more than twenty years of age. She was dressed in brown skins decorated with long strands of colorful beads. The skins hung from her shoulders and fell down to just above her bare feet. It was the traditional dress for all the women of the tribe for such an occasion. Her eyes were dark brown and her hair was long and black and hung down to the middle of her back, braided in colorful beads. Her beauty caught the eye of the young soldiers immediately. LaRouche couldn't help but stare at her as she passed in front of them. His eyes followed her as she walked back to her husband and sat next to him.

The women of the village had prepared a great feast of wild game, poultry and corn. St. Denis knew that the past two summers, including this one, had been harsh all around this part of the country. So he knew that such a grand meal must be a large sacrifice for these people, yet they still offer everything so unselfishly. It should be their honor to accept such a gesture. He learned this very quickly during his travels through the New World among the native peoples. But he also knew it would be an even greater dishonor if they did not accept their offerings of this meal.

They were given a royal welcome. As they ate, they watched the first dance given by Ayita (whose name means, 'first to dance'). This was the dance for rain. A member from each family then came up one at a time to perform a dance for them. The last dance was to call the 'great spirit' to come among them so that they may give thanks to him. It was the most spectacular dance of them all.

As the night grew old, the people began to leave a few at a time and head back to their huts. Each one nodding to the white men still seated on the ground next to Natchitos. St. Denis soon stood up himself and motioned to Buffalo Tamer. He wanted to thank his hosts for their generosity. But before he could speak, Buffalo Tamer spoke to him instead, "Lieutenant, the chief would like to speak with you alone."

St. Denis thought for a moment, then said to Jean-Baptiste, "Sir, please take the men back to the camp, I'll follow you shortly."

"Are you sure that is wise, Louis? Maybe you should wait until tomorrow," Jean-Baptiste insisted.

"No, it will be alright, there is no reason for me to fear," he assured the governor.

"We can wait for you by the river, then," Jean-Baptiste insisted.

"That won't be necessary, Governor. I will have a ride after we talk. Please, take the men back and get some rest."

Jean-Baptiste was not sure about St. Denis' comfort level, he did not think it was wise to be alone with the Indians. But he thought to himself, *"He has spent a great deal of time working with these kinds of people, he must know what he is doing."*

The warrior from the river had come up to the village and was waiting to escort the soldiers and Jean-Baptiste back to their rafts. St. Denis watched as they disappeared into the night.

Chapter 3

St. Denis and Buffalo Tamer followed Natchitos into a small hut, where a fire was lit. St. Denis thought this to be Natchitos' home, but it was not. It was merely a place for the chief to come and smoke and talk with his friends.

Natchitos produced a long leather pouch. He began to unravel the leather strings which were tied around the pouch. He opened the pouch and pulled out an old and long calumet. It was adorned with hawk feathers with different symbols marked on the sides in red and gold paint. He also produced a pouch with tobacco, a rare commodity. He lit the pipe and took a couple of long puffs on it. He exhaled in satisfaction, and then carefully handed the pipe across the fire over to St. Denis. He motioned for him to smoke it as well. St. Denis did as he was shown. Natchitos could see that he was no stranger to sharing a pipe in the company of friends. St. Denis knew he should wait for Natchitos to speak first. Buffalo Tamer waited patiently for his time to translate.

After taking another smoke from the calumet, Natchitos finally spoke, "When I awoke this morning, I saw a dove fly over the rising sun. A dove is always a sign of something new. Now I know why I saw this dove." Buffalo Tamer spoke the exact words to St. Denis in his language.

"I thank you for your generosity, Natchitos," replied St. Denis. "I am humbled by the kindness and hospitality by you and all the people of your tribe. But I am sure you are wondering why we have come here."

"That is why I have asked you here," Natchitos said in return. "Let this smoke signify a peace between you and me. I know you will honor this peace. For I feel that your heart is a good one. Now, what is it that you wish?"

St. Denis responded, "I am a man of peace, and for your offering, I am grateful. I am a wanderer, an explorer. I like to see

28

new lands and new people. I have come to learn from your people. We do not wish to take over your lands and we do not wish to overthrow you. We wish to establish relationships with the tribes all along the river so trade can be promoted. We have goods that we can bring you and skills that we can teach that will help you with your crops and bring prosperity and good life to your people."

Natchitos thought for a moment, and then said, "A wanderer can be a good thing. I know what it means to go and see new places. That is how we have come to live here alongside the river." St. Denis listened to him intently. "What is it that you wish to learn?

"I would like to learn to speak your language," St. Denis answered. "I feel if my communication with you and your people is better, the more progress we can make. It will also help me in understanding and respecting your ways. With your permission, my men can show your people new ways to cultivate land and irrigate your crops. For me, all I wish is to learn your ways, and to learn your language." St. Denis produced a leather pouch of his own from a satchel he had beside him. "With your permission, I would like to honor you with this gift as my thanks to you."

Natchitos looked intrigued. He watched as St. Denis pulled open a button clasp on each end of the pouch. He opened it and revealed a rare and hand-crafted, shiny new flintlock pistol. It was made of polished brown wood and silver steel. The handle was carved with an intricate design in the wood and a rounded, gold tip on the end. The pouch also contained some ammunition made specifically for the pistol and gunpowder wrapped tightly. Natchitos and Buffalo Tamer marveled at the sight. St. Denis was delighted at their curiosity. He handed it over to the chief and let him examine it thoroughly. "It has never been fired," he said. "And, it is yours as a token of my gratitude."

A small grin appeared on the chief's face. "I have seen the white man's rifle, but never have I seen one so small!" He set the pistol down and looked at St. Denis. "I accept your peace. Our men shall work together. And, I personally will help you with our words."

As the days went on, the French and the Indians began to get accustomed to one another. They shared meals, they fished in the river, and even played games with rocks and arrows. But soon the rest and relaxation and blending of cultures was put aside, for there was work to be done. The Indians were in a crucial time of the harvest, and welcomed the extra help in their small corn and bean fields. The harvest was meager compared to years past, but enough to see them through the winter. St. Denis realized that these crops were valuable to the Indians, so he did not want to encroach too much on their hosts and instructed his men to not eat much of what they had harvested.

St. Denis noticed how every morning Natchitos would go up to the top of the hill overlooking the river and would sit and stare out for an hour or more at a time. He wanted to go up and join him but felt it best not to interrupt him. One day he asked Sitting Crow, brother of Tooantuh, why Natchitos climbed and sat on the hill each morning. Sitting Crow explained to St. Denis, "Natchitos is the chief of our tribe, but he is also our spirit guide. He sits on the hill in the rising sun to cleanse his own spirit."

"Has anyone ever gone up there with him?" St. Denis asked.

"No, it is not our place to interrupt the spirit guide when he is alone with his thoughts," Sitting Crow said. St. Denis decided not to push the subject any further.

After the work was done in the fields, Tooantuh asked to form a hunting party. Natchitos readily agreed to the idea. He knew there was ample wild game in the forests. It was common to hunt for deer, hogs, bear, and even buffalo during certain times of the year. The younger braves liked to hunt for small game, such as rabbit, opossum, quail, and squirrels. Tooantuh was eager to show off his hunting skills to the newcomers. His skill with the bow and arrow was unrivaled within the tribe.

One afternoon, he and Sitting Crow, took two of the young braves, LaRouche, and two of the other soldiers on a hunting party. They quietly stalked the forest with Tooantuh in front of the group. He held up his fist, signaling them to halt. He sensed something in the brush a few paces to his right. It was a rabbit! He signaled to the youngest brave, Natchitos' second son, Nito, to take his best aim. But before Nito could strike, he was startled by the blast of a musket. They all turned to see LaRouche standing with a smoking rifle pointed towards the brush.

"Ah, I think I missed him!" muttered LaRouche. Tooantuh and Sitting Crow were dumbfounded on why he would try to kill a rabbit with such a large weapon.

"You missed him!" shouted Nito. "And now you've scared him away." Tooantuh scolded him as well, but LaRouche had no idea what they were saying.

"Gee Sarge, at least let the kid shoot at him first," a young soldier piped up. His name was Etienne Sommer.

"Mind yourself, soldier!" LaRouche stammered. "What's that kid going to use anyway?" motioning to little Nito.

Nito instinctively knew what the sergeant was questioning. He smiled and then pulled out a handful of small wooden arrows, about the six inches in length. Each had a sharp, narrow arrowhead on the tips. They were called hand darts. "This is what you use for a little rabbit, don't you know that?" Nito quipped in his own language. "Not that big noisy thing!" Tooantuh and Sitting Crow both chuckled to themselves. LaRouche was embarrassed and not amused.

A few hours later, the hunters again came across a rabbit. Tooantuh led Nito up to the front once again. The Indians looked back at the soldiers and gave them an obvious look not to interfere this time. LaRouche held up both hands in compliance and a sarcastic smile on his face. Nito took two slow steps forward then crouched down. He slowly took two hand darts from a pouch. He readied one dart in one hand and held the second in his other. He waited for the right moment. The rabbit lifted his head, sensing he had been spotted. He began to jump and scamper away, but it was too late. Two darts split through the air, one after the other and hit their target precisely, *thump, thump!* Nito then stood tall and proud and turned and gave a broad smile in LaRouche's direction. Tooantuh looked on proudly and patted the young brave on his head. "Nice aim, little Nito," he said with a smile. The soldiers applauded in admiration, including the impressed LaRouche.

Back at the village, St. Denis and Natchitos sat in an open area near the river. The sun was warm and it felt good to sit and relax for a while. A swift breeze blew alongside the river as they sat. Buffalo Tamer sat with them as well. "What can I teach you today?" asked Natchitos.

St. Denis held up his hand to Buffalo Tamer, "Let me try and answer him." Buffalo Tamer nodded. St. Denis spoke slowly in the Nashitosh language, one word at a time, "I...seek...learn...Nashitosh...way." Natchitos nodded.

"You learn fast, my friend," Natchitos responded. "In time, you may come to understand our ways, but first you must learn the words and then the purpose behind the words. The winds that blow on a prairie, will stir up clouds to make rain in the river valley. Or they can blow in and dry up the waters. One action can be one or the other. One's purpose is to prepare for the changes that the winds bring forth."

Natchitos took out a small pouch of food and opened it and offered some to St. Denis and Buffalo Tamer. Buffalo Tamer, knowing what it was, took a piece and nodded with a thankful smile. "Here my friend, try this. It is something I like to chew at times like these."

St. Denis was intrigued. He took a piece and put it in his mouth. A smile appeared on his face. It was bagasse, sugar cubes cut from the stalks of cane that grew by the river. He nodded to Natchitos in thanks, "Excellent taste!" Natchitos and Buffalo Tamer were both in agreement.

Natchitos sat and stared at the waters flowing by, then finished his bagasse and spat it out. "Try to say these words, my friend: The wind blows swiftly upon the river today."

St. Denis thought for a few moments, then said slowly, "The...old...river...blows...crazy...today. Is that right?" Natchitos and Buffalo Tamer both laughed at him. "Alright, alright, but no laughing though!"

Chapter 4

It was night and quiet outside the village. The moon was full and bright over the river. The soldiers had gone back to their camp for the night and no one was about the tribal village, except for Natchitos. He was walking along the riverside by the light of the moon. *"Peaceful,"* he thought. He pondered all the new activity that had been happening with the newcomers and with his own family as well. Taima was expecting their fourth child and she had an even heavier burden to bear in the hot summer sun. His responsibility was for her but also for the tribe. The crops yielded little harvest this year and still the rains were not coming. He welcomed the helpfulness of the French but their help could only do so much. He walked along thinking of many things.

He entered his family hut to see Taima and his daughter, now just over four years of age. Her name was Talulah, for she loved to play in the shallow waters. She sat cross-legged in front of her mother who was combing her hair with a wooden comb. Anoki and Nito were fast asleep.

Taima looked up when he walked in, "You are restless this evening." She finished combing Talulah's long hair. "Time for you to go to sleep, little one. Go now." Tallulah crossed her arms and pouted in protest. But then she hopped up and hugged her father's legs. "Good night, Father. Don't make Mother restless too," Talulah said sweetly.

"Sleep well, my little one," Natchitos replied. He sat beside Taima on the grass mat floor.

"You seem troubled this evening, my husband. Tell me what weighs on your mind," Taima said. "What do you think of these white men?" She knew the years of responsibility had taken its toll on Natchitos, but he handled each day without complaint. She was always proud of him and happy that the tribe could live in peace for all these years. But the coming of the white men troubled her as well, although she always tried to see the good in everything.

"I like the Lieutenant very much," Natchitos began. "His curiosity has enlivened my spirit. He has his troubles with his men from time to time, just as I do, but he handles them well. I think he is on the right path. There is no need for our people to fear them. But, other tribes in our land all agree that the white men will keep coming into our land. We will not be able to trust all of them. This is what concerns me."

"You have always been the steady provider for us and our children, and a wise leader for all the Nashitosh," Taima said in response. "I never worry about this. If the whites continue to come, we can not change this. We can only be the people we are. And that is the tribe of the Nashitosh. That will never change."

Natchitos smiled at her. He knew her words would comfort him as usual. "Ah, the true wisdom behind the chief, that you are!" He kissed the top of her forehead. "Let us get some sleep."

"Yes, let us get some sleep," Anoki insisted with his eyes still closed. Taima tried to hold back her laughter as her husband tossed a deer skin blanket at him.

Early the next morning, St. Denis and Jean-Baptiste were standing next to a small bayou that forked from the river towards the west. It was not far from the tribal village. A tall grove of trees stood nearby with ample shade all around.

Jean-Baptiste said, "This would be a good place to build a small structure for the trading post, don't you think, Louis? The land is flat and the stream gives ample room to paddle away from the main river traffic."

"I agree," St. Denis replied. "It is a good spot. But, we must first ask the chief for his permission. I don't know yet how he has taken to the idea of trade with us. He is always reluctant to answer whenever I broach the subject."

"Has he come down yet from his perch today?" Jean-Baptiste quipped.

"Governor, be nice. I admire a man who reserves time for his personal reflection," said St. Denis. "I could use a minute here and there myself, sometimes."

"Monsieur, are you implying something?" Jean-Baptiste said with a wry smile. "But seriously, it would be a good opportunity to show the Indians how to build a more formidable structure and use our modern tools as well."

"I will go and speak with him," St. Denis said. "I am ready to put the men back to work."

By the time they had made it back to the village, Natchitos had descended from the hill where he watched the rising sun. St. Denis had summoned Buffalo Tamer, for he was still not comfortable with his mastery of the Nashitosh language. They approached Natchitos. "Chief, my colleague and I are seeking your permission to build a small hut over by the small bayou downstream."

"Is this where you wish to live?" Natchitos asked curiously.

"No," said St. Denis. "This is where we would like to set up a trading post to be used in the future between us, the French, and your people. This would be the center of trading activity."

"Take me to the site that you have selected," Natchitos replied.

They walked down the river to where the bayou flowed towards the west. They stood in the open area among the tall trees. "Ah, a good choice indeed," Natchitos said. "You have my permission, but there is one thing that I ask of you. I have come to trust you, the French white men. I know your intentions are good. If you pledge to fortify this hut and help me protect my people from any other outsiders, I will let you build this post. This is all I ask."

St. Denis and Jean-Baptiste both readily agreed, as they expected such a response. So Natchitos summoned six of his men to join the soldiers in the building of the post. Jean-Baptiste oversaw the construction of the building. The men and the Indians worked together in cutting down trees and sawing them with tools provided by the soldiers. The Indians learned quickly and were intrigued to see this new way of building. After a few days time, the post had already taken shape. Jean-Baptiste was pleased with their progress.

It was mid-afternoon on the fourth day and the post was near completion. The sun was hot and the hard work had taken its toll. Jean-Baptiste beckoned the men to rest after they had something to eat and drink.

LaRouche and Sommer sat under a large tree dozing in the mid-afternoon. Sommer had his cap pulled over his eyes. "I can't tell you how much this tires me," LaRouche said with his eyes closed. "I don't know why we're bothering with building this shack out in the middle of nowhere. Nobody's going to use this place as a trading post anyway. I know I wouldn't."

"Quiet down, Henri, I'm trying to get some sleep here," Sommer said. "I've got my mind on Lenoire back home."

"Dream away, my friend," LaRouche responded. "I've had enough of this and I don't feel like napping either. I'm going for a walk." So, LaRouche wandered off into the thick grove of trees. He walked with heavy thoughts on his mind. Frustration was growing on him as he thought of his commanding officers barking orders as the men labored away to assist in the construction of the trading post. To him, they were just wasting their time with these people.

He walked a little further and then came upon a footpath. It pointed in the direction of the river. So he followed it until it came up to a bend. He started to slow down as he could hear the sound of the water. He could also hear the sound of women laughing. He stepped off into the brush and crouched down and slowly crept forward to try and see where the laughter was. He stretched his head out as far as he could and finally he saw them. Two Indian women were bathing in the river. They were in the water, with their backs turned toward him, laughing and enjoying the cool waters. LaRouche smiled at how his fortune had changed for the better and so quickly. The younger of the two women turned her head slightly. He could see her face now and saw that it was the beautiful young girl from the first night, Ayita. This was his chance he thought, his chance to make this journey worthwhile.

He stood up slightly and took one step forward, when suddenly an arrow zipped in front of him and pierced the tree right next to him. LaRouche fell back startled. He stepped back clumsily, tripping over a rock and fell to the ground. The women grew silent when they heard the noise behind them. LaRouche tried to scramble to his feet but Tooantuh jumped down from a nearby tree and pinned him to the ground as he pointed a spear at his chest.

"This place is forbidden to white men!" Tooantuh said angrily. "You must not be here!" Ayita and Taima were stunned at the intrusion. They remained in the water and watched warily behind the cover of a tree log.

"Hey, I was just seeing what the noise was in the water," LaRouche said innocently. Tooantuh dug the spear deeper into his chest. "Hey, watch it! Let me go!"

Tooantuh stood over him with a glare. LaRouche knew he was in trouble. He lay there silently staring back at Tooantuh. Tooantuh pulled the spear away and let him stand up. "You must never come to this place again," he said still angry. "Go! Away with you!"

Tooantuh turned to walk away but LaRouche bent down and pulled a dagger from his boot, "You should have never let me up," LaRouche muttered under his breath. He lunged towards Tooantuh with the dagger but stopped in mid-air when he heard the sound of several bows being pulled taut right behind him. He slowly turned around and saw four braves pointing arrows directly at him. Tooantuh stood glaring at him in victorious defiance. LaRouche dropped the dagger at his feet and held up his hands. Tooantuh motioned to the braves and they lowered their arrows. With that, LaRouche ran like the wind towards the village.

LaRouche ran all the way back to the building site. He ran past the trees where Sommer was resting. He stopped beside a large oak tree trying to catch his breath, leaning on one arm against the tree.

"What happened to you? Why the devil are you running so fast?" asked Sommer. LaRouche was dripping with sweat. Sommer looked at his friend as if he'd gone mad.

"Nothing, leave me alone," LaRouche said, gasping for air. He stumbled along the path towards the building site. The long rest break was over and the men were resuming their work. He tried to act casually and picked up a wooden hammer and began working feverishly. He didn't want to let on that anything had happened. But he was always looking over his shoulder after that.

At the same time, the new post was taking shape and was nearing completion. Jean-Baptiste stood studying the building plans, and nodded his approval. Then he heard a voice behind him from a distance, "Governor!" It was St. Denis, walking up the path with Natchitos. "How is the post coming along?"

"Splendidly," Jean-Baptiste said with a smile. "The men work well together, it is almost completed. What do you think, Louis?" The men took a small break to admire their work along with the officers and the chief. Natchitos commended his tribesmen on their hard work. LaRouche spotted Tooantuh, and two of the other braves he had encountered earlier, coming down the river from the opposite way. He tried to hide his face and the uneasy feeling that was growing within him. He knew the incident would be reported soon, if not already. However, Taima and Ayita were not with them. They were escorted quietly to the village by another way.

"This is excellent work they have done, Governor. You should be pleased," St. Denis said in admiration. He patted him on the back and Jean-Baptiste nodded in agreement.

It had been two months now since they had landed on the banks of the Cane. Firm roots had been established with the Nashitosh Indians. St. Denis and Jean-Baptiste were more than pleased with their progress and came to like the Indians and admired them greatly for their determination and for their generosity. St. Denis did not, however, want to overstay his welcome here. He knew the soldiers had grown weary and were eager to return to their life at Fort St. Jean.

That night, St. Denis made his way toward the village and approached the warrior standing guard by the river. He asked if he could speak with Natchitos. He spoke in the Nashitosh language, which impressed the warrior. He walked with St. Denis up to the open area where the fire dances were held. "Wait here," he said to St. Denis.

A few moments later, Natchitos appeared from the village. "What do I owe this unexpected visit, Lieutenant?" he asked.

St. Denis had come unaccompanied so that he might test his knowledge of the language alone. "I was wondering if I could speak to you," St. Denis responded. "I wish to tell you of our plans." Natchitos motioned to him to follow him into his smoking hut. They sat down across from each other in front of

40

the fire. *"There always seems to be a fire burning in this hut,"* St. Denis thought to himself.

Natchios spoke, "Some of your words are wrong, but you are learning well." He pulled out his calumet from the long leather pouch. "I was thinking of having a smoke tonight, so I am glad you came. A good smoke and a good fire are always best shared." St. Denis smiled and nodded in agreement. He lit the calumet and took a few long puffs on it, then handed it over to St. Denis. "What would you like to talk about this evening, my friend?"

St. Denis continued in Natchitos' language with broken words, but well enough to understand, "It is time for me and my men to return to the fort. We thank you for letting us live in your lands these last few months." Natchitos said nothing, but kept smoking on the pipe. "We must go back for more supplies and give my soldiers some rest. But with your permission, I would like to return and start to promote trade in this area at the post we have built." Natchitos passed him the pipe as if he had not heard anything St. Denis had said. St. Denis took a few short puffs on the pipe, but waited impatiently for a response.

"The 'great spirit' has taught me many things," Natchitos began. "I see wisdom in opening our minds to learn different ways. I am grateful that my people have learned about your ways. The way of the peaceful man is the way of a just man. I see this in you." He took the pipe from St. Denis and took a few last puffs from it. "I do not know of this place where you live. Where is it that you will go? Do you live with Indians there as well?"

St. Denis did not expect this question. He thought carefully before answering. "Our fort is a little more than a week of travel downstream. It is about two days traveling on the Red, then at least four more days traveling on the Great River. There is a tribe, the Acolapissa, from which we have bought land. They allowed us to build our settlement on this land, as our fort and base." St. Denis thought for a moment. He wondered if he had said too much. But he wanted to be honest with his new friend.

"You truly are an adventurer, Lieutenant St. Denis. Your travels are an inspiration," Natchitos said with a grin. "Good stories to share at the fire at night. My people will not forget you, nor will I. I wish you well on your journey. But, I will cast a hawk's eye on the hill to watch for your return."

St. Denis smiled at his thoughtfulness. "Thank you, Great Chief. You are my friend and you have my word that I will return. I see great possibilities for you and your people. I will make your kindness known." They smoked for a while longer until the tobacco was gone.

Early the next morning, the soldiers and Buffalo Tamer had already packed their camp and loaded both the rafts. St. Denis and Jean-Baptiste stood on the banks of the Cane River while several tribesmen looked on. Natchitos stepped forth from the crowd and approached St. Denis. He held out his right hand and St. Denis clasped his right arm into his in the customary handshake. "Go with the 'great spirit'," Natchitos said with sincerity.

Tooantuh stood among the crowd eyeing LaRouche sitting in one of the rafts. LaRouche sat and glared back at him. He knew what Tooantuh must be thinking. He was lucky to be leaving while he could. *"Had he reported to the chief what he had done?"* he thought to hiimself. LaRouche grew even more impatient and paranoid, not knowing what consequences he would face.

Jean-Baptiste and St. Denis boarded the rafts and they pushed off from the banks. They turned and paddled their rafts away from the Indians. One by one, the Indians turned and walked back to the village. All had left except for Natchitos, who was now sitting up on the hill in his usual morning spot. He watched the rafts until they disappeared from sight.

Chapter 5

Winter arrived in a fury that year. It was very harsh, more so than in years past. The tribe did their best to keep everyone warm with pelts and blankets that were given to them by the French. Few braved the cold and food began to dwindle. On certain days when the sun would peak from the clouds, Tooantuh would make his way down to the river to try his luck at fishing. He would catch only scarce amounts of fish. The winter never seemed to end this year, and it weighed heavy on the mind of the chief.

Taima was entering her last month and knew at any time she could give birth to her baby. When any woman went into labor in the village, she was the one who came to aid with the delivery. But this time, she was the one in need of help.

Early in the cold night, Taima sat silently in the hut with Natchitos and their three children around a small fire. The cold wind blew fiercely outside, and no one dared to step out. They were all huddled together trying to stay warm. Natchitos stared into the fire for moments at a time, drifting off to sleep as he sat upright. The heavy animal skins wrapped tightly around each of them were enough to nearly hold one in place in a sitting position without much effort. Nito and Talulah giggled at the sight of their father napping as he sat. Taima raised her finger to her lips to quiet them. Just then, her eyes flew wide open and she cried out in pain. Natchitos awakened to the sound of her labor pains. The children looked up at her with alarm. Talulah was afraid to see her mother in such pain.

"Anoki, go and summon Ayita!" Taima cried in agony. "Tell her to come with water." Anoki arose immediately and ran to fetch Ayita. Natchitos helped Taima to the bed of thick animal pelts spread on the ground, trying to calm her. He sat by the fire next to Talulah and Nito and tried to calm them as well.

"It is alright, soon you will have a new brother or sister," he said to the children. Talulah's eyes lit up. "I hope it's a sister!" she said enthusiastically.

Ayita showed up only minutes later with Anoki following behind her, carrying two skins full of water. "I will need more water. Go to the river and fill what you can," she instructed Anoki. He did as she said and soon there were six skins full of water for her. Anoki sat huddled together with his father and his little brother and sister. Taima continued to cry out in pain as the labor became more intense. Ayita cooled her head with a damp cloth made of fox hide. She tried to keep Taima as calm as she could. But Taima grew more restless. Her eyes opened between the contractions and pain and saw all her family sitting around the fire trying to keep warm. The hut was small so it was somewhat crowded with all six of them inside. Taima's impatience grew to an end. She wailed out in pain again and lunged forward and glared at Natchitos. "A mass meeting now, is it? Out! All of you!" she snapped.

Ayita agreed. She stood and motioned quickly to Natchitos and the three children to leave quickly. "Go, go! Leave us now." Natchitos did not argue. The next minute he and the three children were all cramped inside the small smoking hut huddling together for warmth. Not a word was said as they sat listening to the howling wind in the chill of the night.

Taima had the hut to her own now and started to calm down, but the contractions continued for several hours. Ayita stayed at her side the entire time, trying to keep her head cool. Even though the air was freezing outside, Taima's forehead sweated profusely. From time to time, Natchitos could hear his wife's pain coming from the hut next door. He stayed awake all of the night worrying about her. The children did their best to try and sleep in the cramped hut.

The blustery wind continued to blow throughout the night. Hours had passed and the small fire had become just a small flame. Next door, Natchitos stared at the embers in the fire bed in front of him. The fire had gone out. At first light he would go out to find dry wood to build both fires back up again. Suddenly, he heard a faint cry. But this time it was not of his wife, but that of a baby. It was near sunrise when the baby had been born.

Natchitos lifted himself up, trying not to stir the children. Anoki looked up at him with bleary eyes. "Stay here with them," he said to Anoki. He stepped outside into the cold. It was still mostly dark but a glow to the east was visible now as the sunrise approached. The wind had finally calmed down. He pulled aside the animal skin door slightly to his home and peered inside. Ayita sat stirring what was left of the fire. Behind her lay Taima, exhausted. She held close to her breast a tiny baby boy. The baby's eyes were closed, too weary to open them after the long ordeal. "I will go get fresh wood for the fire," Natchitos said quietly. Before he turned to go out, he looked at Ayita and said to her, "Thank you." She nodded at him.

On the third day, the entire tribe came together to hold a gathering at the tribal fire. Dances were performed as a sign of welcome and blessings of a long and fruitful life for the tribe's newest arrival. At the same time, a name was given to the baby. Despite the cold, all of the tribe attended and a great fire was built in the center of the village. Each family performed a dance in honor of the newborn baby. Makane, the oldest member of the tribe, stood and spoke.

"The 'great spirit' has given us a new life. We dance to give thanks for this gift to the Nashitosh. And, we dance for the spring to give us new life in our fields. Now, let a new name be spoken." He motioned towards Taima and Natchitos.

Taima held her baby boy closely in her arms. He was wrapped warmly and his eyes were wide open, taking in the

46

spectacle around him. Taima spoke, "He came into this world in the cold wind of the night, so he will be called Aykwa Unule (which means 'cold wind')." From then on, he was known simply as Nule.

A few weeks later, early in the cold morning, tragedy struck the village. Makane had passed away during the night. Makane was known as a wise man and the medicine man of the village. He had lived a long life. The entire tribe mourned his death. A dance was performed amid the fire in hopes his spirit would rise up with the burning embers and smoke. The tribal custom for the funeral was not to bury the body. A member of the family was responsible for taking the body away from the village and placed alone, far out into the forest. They believed that once wild animals came along to discard the body, the spirit would be allowed to go free and pass on to the next life. This is why they did not bury their dead. Makane was taken into the forest by his oldest son, and was left alone. They mourned him for three days.

As winter slowly gave way to spring, the Indians were more than happy to feel the warmer air. Life began to return to the trees and flowers in the groves. And more animals began to appear from the woods. It was a long and harsh winter for the Nashitosh, and now they had to prepare the lands for this summer's crops. Little corn and beans were yielded in the previous year, so there was little seed to begin this year. The rains still had not come when spring began, so a long dry summer was in store for them once again.

Tooantuh and his hunters took to the forests in search of wild game, but were only able to find a few small rabbits and opossums. The dry weather had led the larger wildlife away from the area.

Natchitos could see that they had become in more dire need of food than ever before. With the warmer weather, he had expected to see the explorers coming down the river with much needed supplies. *"We cannot rely on the white men to come and help us,"* Natchitos thought to himself. *"We have survived hardships in the past, so we must endure this one as well."* But he did wish to see his friend St. Denis once again. He had thought of him many times since their departure last fall. He wondered of his progress with the Acolapissa.

The days grew warmer and very little rain fell and the crop land was dry and dusty. They had planted what seed they had but little hope was held for the crops to bear ample food. They lived on small fish and a few small forest animals that they could hunt. Spring became summer and the French still had not returned. *"Why would they build this post and then leave it to crumble and rot?"* Natchitos asked himself. *"Why do they not return?"* He stood along the bayou and stared at the fort that had been built. No one had entered the structure the entire time it stood there. They waited for the French to return and put it to use. But the fort had fallen into disrepair over the long harsh winter, and showed signs of neglect. Tooantuh had been hunting when he noticed the chief standing by the fort.

"The whites are not returning as they promised," he said sternly. "They must have decided they can not live in this land."

"No," said Natchitos, "I sense they must have trouble. They had a purpose here and I don't think they would abandon their plans so quickly. Something has happened."

"We cannot worry about their problems," Tooantuh retorted. "We have to solve our own here. We should tear this down and use the wood." He walked off shaking his head. His frustration was obvious.

Natchitos knew that something had to be done soon or his people may starve. One morning, Anoki came running into the village, "Father, Father! Come quick!" He was very excited as usual and animated in trying to beckon his father to follow him to the fields.

Natchitos hurried behind his anxious son and followed him into the corn fields. "Look Father, they are growing!" Anoki said with a broad smile. Indeed, the corn had begun to sprout. A few light rains had fallen in the prior days. It was all the rain they had received in months. Natchitos felt this was a sign of hope that things had finally turned for the better. He shared the news with Taima and the rest of the tribe. Hope had been restored, at least for a while.

The days grew hotter and the rain had stopped. But the corn had grown to about two feet by then. But food was still scarce and activity around the village had all but stopped. They tried to stay cool along the banks of the Cane, but hunger overwhelmed any sense of temporary relief from the heat.

Late one afternoon, Tooantuh ran up the slopes to take a look at the corn fields. He fell to his knees when he saw the fields. All the corn had wilted and fell to the ground and was covered with dust and dried mud. The crop was ruined from the heat. He could not pull himself up. His sadness and weariness enveloped him.

Back in the village, Taima sat in the shade, combing Talulah's hair. Nule lay fast asleep, nestled in a pile of animal pelts. Natchitos sat nearby leaning against a large rock with his eyes closed. Taima looked up to the sound of approaching footsteps. She gasped loudly and Natchitos looked up startled. There stood Tooantuh, holding a wilted corn stalk that he had uprooted. "It's all gone," he said wearily. Then he dropped it on the ground. Natchitos' heart sank in his chest. He knew what must be done.

Chapter 6

It was late summer, in 1702, at Fort St. Jean. There was much activity about the fort as this was the busiest time of year. Traders were coming down the Great River (which was also called the Colbert River by the French) in large numbers with pelts and food to trade.

Life was busy for the French officers, for the task of keeping the Spanish explorers out of their territory was a daily chore. The Acolapissa Indians were not as accommodating to the French as they had been in the past as well. Their demands increased as time went on. Despite this, St. Denis continued to press Governor Bienville to let him take some men back up to the head of the Red River to establish the trading routes in that area. Jean-Baptiste knew that this was a key area in the trade routes, having seen this area for himself, but he could not afford to spare any men in these hectic days.

The fort was situated on the northern banks of the river. The Acolapissa Indians were situated on the shores of Lake Pontchartrain. The explorers had to travel a few miles north on narrow bayous that ran through rugged and murky swamplands to get to the village. The Indians were regular visitors to the fort for trade with the settlers. A good relationship had been established between them and the French in the early days, but now they began to resent the ever growing number of white traders and settlers in the area.

Fog was common in these waters of the lower delta, the air was very humid and hot and mosquitoes were a common problem as well. On this morning, the fog was very thick upon the river. St. Denis was checking provisions for the troops that were preparing to head west in the following days. A garrison was prepared to setup front lines to the west to counter the Spanish incursion.

He walked outside the main gate of the fort, when he heard a call from atop the lookout, "A column is ahead! River upstream!" St. Denis climbed to a higher position to get a better look. It was difficult to see through the fog, but as they came closer, he could see twenty or more canoes coming down the river, each with two to four Indians aboard. "Take your positions, men! Be at the ready!" was the call from the lookout. At the head of the group, St. Denis could make out an Indian wearing a familiar headdress. As they neared, his eyes widened in disbelief.

"Hold your fire! Hold your fire!" he shouted to the lookout. The sentry in the lookout obeyed and shouted down the line, "Hold your fire!" St. Denis rushed to the ground, flung open the main gate, and ran towards the river. It was Natchitos at the head of the group of canoes. He was followed by the entire Nashitosh tribe.

Natchitos neared the fort and he saw a man waving his arms from the shore. He recognized him at once as St. Denis. The column of canoes came ashore, one by one, lined up like marshals along the shores of the Great River. Natchitos and Taima stepped out of the canoe and walked towards St. Denis. Taima held Nule close in her arms. "Lieutenant, I am Natchitos, I have come to your land," Natchitos said.

"Yes!" he exclaimed. "Yes, I know it is you. Welcome, my friend. Welcome to all of you. You have traveled a long way. Please come and we will give you food and water." He noticed the baby in Taima's arms, now about eight months old. "You have added to your family, I see. This is wonderful to see, my friend."

Another officer, Colonel Jean-Pierre Lemont, approached from the fort, seeing this great number of Indians coming ashore. "Lieutenant, what is going on here? Who are these people?" he demanded.

"Not to worry, Sir. I know this man from the Red River area." St. Denis explained. "They are not a threat to us, Sir."

"But why are they here? There must be more than sixty or seventy of them!" Lemont persisted. "Ask them why they are here, right away."

"I will, Sir, I will find out why they are here," St. Denis answered. "But first let's give them some food and rest. They have been traveling for many days. I know how far they have come."

"Take care of it quickly, Louis, I don't want them all over this fort," Lemont instructed him. "There is too much work to be done around here as it is."

"Yes, Sir."

Many of the soldiers were now looking on at this amazing sight. Many of the Indians appeared frightened, they had never seen this many white men before at one time. They stood closely together and avoided staring at the soldiers.

Among the soldiers upon the fort was LaRouche. He walked between a few men who were closer and had a better vantage point. He shoved his head forward between the two men and glared down at the group of Indians along the river. "Well I'll be damned!" he said in disbelief. "He brought back the whole damn bunch of them!" The other men looked at him quizzically and gave him a laugh. *They've come back to get me,* he thought to himself. His mind had eased over the past year but no longer. He did not like the sight of these Indians at all.

St. Denis sat in the governor's chamber inside of Fort St. Jean. Jean-Baptiste sat behind a desk wearing the traditional wig. "I understand we have some visitors with us today, eh Louis?"

"Yes, Governor. They are being given some food and water at this very moment," answered St. Denis.

"Do you know why they are here?"

"No Sir, but I get the feeling they are not here just to say hello. I'm afraid something must have happened to them, or the whole tribe would not have come along with the chief."

"How many do they number?" Jean-Baptiste asked.

"From my estimates, about fifty men, women and children, Sir."

"And what do you suppose that we do with our friends that have shown up so unexpectedly?" asked Jean-Baptiste sarcastically. "I understand their position is dire, but we do not have the capacity to put up such a large number of refugees, no matter what their circumstances."

"I understand, Sir. They can not stay here." St. Denis sat quietly for a moment. Then he raised his hand to his chin. "But there is ample room north of here on the lake," St. Denis thought aloud.

"Are you sure that is wise, monsieur?" asked Jean-Baptiste. "The natives along that lake are hardly pleased with us as it is now. I'd hate to see their reaction if we relocate this tribe alongside them. They'll want even more in return for certain."

"Yes," thought St. Denis. "But it seems we have very few options. I think if we gather up enough provisions to bring the Acolapissa, it's possible it will be enough of an offering to allow the Nashitosh to stay and share the lakeshore. After all, it is a large lake."

"Indeed, but territory is a touchy subject with the natives," Jean-Baptiste cautioned. "Don't forget what it took to acquire the land we hold now." He thought for a few moments more. "You have my permission, Louis, do what you can."

St. Denis gathered up a team of soldiers and instructed them to put provisions together, including food, blankets, animal pelts and grains to bring to the Acolapissa. Sergeant LaRouche was the leader of the small platoon of soldiers. He was not amused on that he had been pulled back into duty helping this tribe once again. St. Denis also summoned Andre Pénicaut, an honorable man and carpenter whom he trusted. He placed him in charge of leading the displaced Nashitosh tribe to Lake Pontchartrain. St. Denis would travel with them initially to help them get settled.

He and Pénicaut approached a small area outside the fort where the Nashitosh were gathered. They were given food and they sat quietly and ate their first meal in days. St. Denis spotted Natchitos sitting with his family and walked towards them. Natchitos saw him coming, so he stood to greet him.

"Tell me my friend, are you fleeing some type of danger?" he asked Natchitos.

Natchitos explained, "I saw that you were not coming, so I thought you had trouble. I thought of sending a party to come and give you aid. But the crops became lost and my people were restless and weakened. I could not send my men any longer. I am sorry."

"There is no need to apologize," St. Denis responded. "I am honored by your gesture. Please accept my apologies for not returning to your area sooner. I did not know the situation with your crops had become so desperate. You made a wise decision in coming here. I will help you as much as I can."

He then introduced Pénicaut to Natchitos. "Monsieur Pénicaut is a builder, and a trusted friend. He has agreed to go with you to the lake that is nearby. There you and your people can settle and live without fear." Natchitos nodded to Pénicaut. "But my friend, there is another tribe at the lake, the Acolapissa. This is the tribe of which I spoke to you. We obtained this land from them." Natchitos nodded in understanding. "I know the chief of this tribe, he is called Red Hawk. He is a good man, but he is a cautious man as well. It may take some time for him to be comfortable with new neighbors. Do you understand?"

Natchitos looked at him with confidence. "We are in your debt, Lieutenant. I thank you. I will meet this Chief Red Hawk. It is I who should ask for his permission." St. Denis and

Pénicaut looked at each other with some worry. But St. Denis trusted his instincts. He nodded to Natchitos in agreement.

The tribe began to gather and load into their canoes. The soldiers pulled their boats alongside the canoes to load more provisions. LaRouche stood at the bow of one boat and barked orders at the men. They handed him crates one by one. As he worked, LaRouche scanned over the tribe with a glare. The he saw him. Tooantuh was loading a canoe just fifteen yards downstream. He kept his eyes fixed on him as he worked. Then Tooantuh sensed he was being watched, and he looked up to see LaRouche staring at him. He stopped what he was doing and walked a few paces towards LaRouche and stopped.

"What are you looking at, Sarge?" asked the young soldier handing him crates. Tooantuh glanced at Ayita, then back at LaRouche.

"Nothing soldier, hand me that crate! Let's keep it moving!" he shouted. Tooantuh turned back and climbed into his canoe with Ayita.

The tribe set out and followed St. Denis, Pénicaut, and the soldiers up a small bayou towards Lake Pontchartrain. It was no more than an hour's journey. St. Denis grew nervous, for he did not know how this encounter with the Acolapissa would unfold.

The landscape was quite different to the Nashitosh. There were marshes and bayous all around. It seemed like you could go anywhere by canoe. There was more water than there was land. Rains fell more often and the air was always thick with humidity. As they entered a clearing from the trees, their eyes widened with amazement. They had come upon the great lake. They had never seen such a large body of water before. The lake stretched to the horizon as far as the eye could see. Gulls flew overhead, a kind of bird which they had never seen either. Up towards the west shore, a tribal village could be seen. Many grass and thatch huts and some more modern wooden huts lined the shore and inland for a few hundred yards. The tribe was relatively small but the village was widespread.

They went as far as they could on the bayou, then they unloaded the canoes and began to walk a short distance. A noise could be heard from the village, as they had spotted the intruders coming down the shore. Natchitos instructed his tribe to find a place to sit and wait while he went to speak to Chief Red Hawk.

Pénicaut knew the language of the Acolapissa, so he walked along with Natchitos and St. Denis towards the village. Five Indians approached them from the village, including Chief Red Hawk. They were all adorned with tattoos on their arms and chests. Each brave had tattoos that depicted accomplishments in battle and the type of warrior they were. They stopped about twenty yards from the two white men and Natchitos. Chief Red Hawk stood in the middle and raised his right hand motioning them to stop. They did as he indicated. Pénicaut spoke in their language, "Greetings to you, Red Hawk, this tribe comes to you in peace."

"Who is this tribe?" asked Red Hawk. "Why do you bring them to me?" He glared at St. Denis and Natchitos intently.

"They are the Nashitosh. They come from the North and are in need of land in which to live. We ask if they may share the lands of the lake with you and your people." Pénicaut explained. "We have brought offerings to you from the fort for your trouble." He pointed towards the boats where the provisions were stowed. Red Hawk looked past them to see the boats where LaRouche and the soldiers were unloading the provisions. He said nothing. Pénicaut instructed the soldiers to bring up the provisions to where they were standing. St. Denis helped LaRouche pile them on the ground in front of Red Hawk.

"We have no need for these offerings," Red Hawk said abruptly. "What you ask of me is land and part of this lake for these strangers to live upon. Why should I grant you this request?" St. Denis was afraid this would be the response.

Natchitos then stepped forward and said to Pénicaut and St. Denis, "Let me speak." He walked closer to Red Hawk and stopped in front of him. He knew the best way to work with another chief was to speak to him directly. This is what Chief Red Hawk expected all along. Pénicaut and St. Denis stood a few feet behind and helped translate for Natchitos.

"I am Natchitos, chief. My people have come down from the North," he explained. "They have suffered many hardships. We come now to seek the great chief's acceptance so that we may dwell here and live in peace." Natchitos then pulled out a small leather pouch. St. Denis looked curiously at it for it seemed familiar. Natchitos removed the clasps on the pouch and opened it. Inside the pouch was the flintlock pistol that was given to him by St. Denis. It had never been fired. The ammunition and gunpowder remained inside the pouch. He lifted the pistol and showed it to Red Hawk. He now had his attention. Red Hawk and his men looked at the pistol with obvious curiosity and interest. Natchitos handed the pistol to Red Hawk and let him examine it.

LaRouche stood with a crooked stare as he looked on. He looked over at St. Denis, then back at Red Hawk holding the pistol. *"So that's how he gets these savages to trust him,"* he thought to himself. LaRouche was beside himself with anger and jealousy. Such a pistol was rare even to an enlisted man. *"How dare he give it to one of these Indians,"* he thought to himself. *"And now this damn Indian is giving it to another!"*

St. Denis felt a little uneasy in seeing the gift he had given to Natchitos being used in such a manner, but he thought, *'It's his gift. He can do what he wants with it."* Furthermore, he could see that this was working better than any of the offerings that he had brought. He quickly decided that this was a very clever gesture.

Natchitos placed the pistol back in the leather pouch and closed it. With the pouch in both hands, he lifted it and offered it to Red Hawk. Red Hawk accepted the pistol and said, "You and your people can live among us here. We will smoke as brothers tonight at the fire." St. Denis and Pénicaut were relieved.

Pénicaut began to help the Nashitosh build living quarters. The Indians used their skills from the year before at their old village and helped him with the tree cutting and construction. Pénicaut had done this with the Acolapissa. The new village was situated about a half mile further down the shore on Lake Pontchartrain from the Acolapissa. As the weeks and months went by, the Nashitosh became more familiar with the new landscape and ways of hunting and fishing in these different waters. Soon, all the tribal families had a place to call home. Natchitos was grateful to Pénicaut for his thankless and ceaseless help that he gave the tribe. Tooantuh and Sitting Crow took to the new wilderness easily and began to hunt the wildlife in the area around the lake with renewed vigor. The two tribes worked together in sowing the nearby fields and planting crops.

The French would send patrols to the area to check on the Indians on a regular basis. Many times, LaRouche lead these patrols as they came through to each village. The Indians now had plenty of game to hunt and ample fish to catch in the lake. When the troops came through, the tribal women would cook meals for them in thanks for their security.

Natchitos soon found a quiet place along the lake to sit and reflect as the sun rose each morning. It wasn't quite the same as his old place up on the hill overlooking the Cane River, but it was sufficient. He treasured his quiet time immensely as the sun rose each morning and it helped him gather the strength to face each coming day.

As the years went by, Natchitos watched his children grow beside the lake. Anoki grew into a strong young brave who became a master hunter and fisherman. Nito and Talulah both started to grow up as well and Natchitos was pleased to see them playing with the other children. And then there was Nule, the last of his tribe to be born at their old village. He started to take his first steps beside the light of the lake and the setting sun. Natchitos was pleased with his tribe's transition, but he longed to be back in his homeland. There was so much more activity around this area, much more than he had ever witnessed. He saw that the white man truly was coming from many directions and it didn't seem like it was going to end. They were all around this area. And not just his tribe, but the Acolapissa were being driven to more and more remote areas, away from their original homes. But his case was different, he thought. He longed for the calming quiet waters of the Cane and his private times of reflection up on the hillside. The Cane River valley was always kind to him and his people and it provided all that they needed. But the years of drought were too much for one man to bear. He thought that the rains would soon return and they would be able to return as well. Yet, he did not know when that time would come for his people. So he was content to hope and pray for this each and every day. His hope was for his youngest son, Nule, and for all his people, to one day return home to the lands of the Cane.

Chapter 7
1713 - Eight Years Later

The French colony began to evolve and the influx of settlers from the old world was ever increasing as the years passed. The colony was assigned a new governor that came from Quebec and Detroit. His name was Antoine Laumet sieur de Cadillac. St. Denis had been sent to nearby Biloxi to help fortify the French fort established there but soon was summoned back to Fort St. Jean by Governor Cadillac. Cadillac was aware of St. Denis' earlier expeditions north of the colony and was now convinced that it was imperative to establish forts in that area for trading and to post soldiers there to keep the Spanish incursion from spreading east from Texas.

Meanwhile, LaRouche had been elevated to the rank of Lieutenant and commanded a group of soldiers at the fort that still patrolled the surrounding area, including the tribal areas on Lake Pontchartrain. Trading continued with the Indians and some of them had even been given muskets for more protection.

The Nashitosh and Acolapissa continued to live alongside one another on the lake but the latter had become somewhat resentful of the newcomers that had arrived and started hunting their game and catching their fish. They complained to the French that the wildlife was no longer plentiful. Tensions had started to rise between the two tribes and they spent less and less time in each other's company.

Early one morning, LaRouche set out on patrol with his company that also included Etienne Sommer, now promoted to Sergeant. "These damn mosquitoes are tough this year, Sergeant," he complained to Sommer. The rain fell hard on the patrol as they sloshed their way through the marsh. "Another few months of this and I'm liable to go nuts. We need to do something."

"About the mosquitoes, Sir?" asked Sommer.

"No, you fool. We need to do something about this lousy detail," he retorted. "We're out here in the heat and mosquitoes while the other brass is up at the fort sipping tea and deciding what the next move is against the Spaniards. *We* should be up there, I'm telling you. What do they know? But, we're stuck down here babysitting these damn Indians." The rain lightened, so they stopped the patrol and decided to start a small fire to keep the mosquitoes at bay.

"I don't know, Henri," Sommer started, "We keep giving them those muskets, but if you ask me we shouldn't have given them any at all. What if they decide to revolt against us? There is only a few of us here at a time while the rest of our men are fighting Spaniards."

"Yes, you're right, my friend. They have too many guns already." LaRouche said as he sat thinking. "Every time I walk around there I think one of them is going to take a shot at me just for the hell of it."

"Ah, you're being paranoid, Lieutenant," Sommer said. "There must be a way to get off this detail and get our tails up to the real fight. I've had it with this patrol, too."

"Yes, there must be a way," LaRouche kept thinking aloud. He sat and stared at the fire for what seemed an eternity. His nostrils flared a little as his thoughts raced. He took a deep breath and cocked his head towards Sommer. "I think I know how."

It was a balmy September morning when St. Denis entered the compound of a bustling Fort St. Jean. The journey from Biloxi was arduous, but good progress had been made there. He was somewhat surprised to see so much activity at the fort. So much more than in years past. This part of the country was no longer a secret. He walked up the steps that led to the governor's office. As he entered, the governor's aide stood at tension, then said, "Please enter, Sir, he is expecting you."

He opened the door to see Cadillac staring out his office window. "Ah, Louis! Welcome back, my friend. I trust your journey went well. May I offer you some tea?

"Yes, thank you, Governor," said St. Denis, standing at the head of a long desk. "It is good to be back, Sir."

"Please, have a seat," Cadillac said as he sat behind the long desk. He poured some hot water into a tea cup for St. Denis and handed it to him. "The winds of change are among us, my friend. For better or for worse, I am not yet certain. The Spaniards are now aware of this place and are very keen in having a share of it. We're finding it much more difficult to hold them back from their locations west of here. I feel a new strategy is needed now."

"I understand, Sir. What are you proposing?" St. Denis asked.

"Tell me about the Red River territory, Commander," Cadillac said directly. "I understand you were very fond of this area, from your reports."

"Yes Sir," replied St. Denis. "The area has a variety of climate changes, fertile soils, and many tributaries that branch from the Red. I was impressed with the different terrain, which is much different than what we are accustomed to here."

"And, those tributaries are quite ample and run in many directions, do they not?" Cadillac asked.

"Yes, Sir. They do."

"In strategic directions, wouldn't you say?" Cadillac continued. "Enough to fortify with posts all along the river to protect the borders?"

St. Denis understood well what the governor was proposing. He looked at him with intrigue. The governor stood and walked over to the window to gaze out again. St. Denis sat, staring at his back. "I understand you befriended one of the native chiefs from that area on your journey over a decade ago," Cadillac said quietly.

"Why yes, that is true," St. Denis said.

"His tribe knows the area quite well, don't they?"

"Well, yes, it was their home, Sir," St. Denis said, looking ashamed after remembering he had not returned as he had promised, so many years ago now. "But, they relocated from that area. They are now living alongside the lake with the Acolapissa. They have for many years now. I'm afraid they encountered some rough conditions in those final years. Something, I did not foresee."

Cadillac continued, "I have sent a scouting patrol up the river to see this area that you described in your journals. They returned this past week and I have word from them that it lush and green and full of promise as you spoke. They saw no more signs of the drought that pressed the Nashitosh to retreat from there."

"Really?" asked St. Denis. He was intrigued. "That is very good news, Governor."

"I have an assignment for you, Louis," Cadillac said as he turned around to face him. "What would you say if I asked you to go back to this area and establish a fort, as you had once planned?" St. Denis began to answer, but Cadillac interupted him by raising his hand. "*And,* take the Nashitosh with you, since they know the land so well."

"What would Red Hawk say to that?" St. Denis asked, knowing this would surely cause more tension among the tribes.

"I know of their quarreling," Cadillac answered. "I'm afraid it is becoming a nuisance that my predecessors did not foresee. I will make an agreement with Chief Red Hawk to give them more land around the lake and also a safe migration route to the Houma tribe if they wish to do so. I understand they have a sound friendship with the Houma. All we will ask in return is that he let the Nashitosh leave in peace."

He had St. Denis' full attention. He had been looking for a way to make amends with Natchitos and his people. He knew they had left unwillingly the land that they loved. He knew this for certain.

"Do you think the Nashitosh would be agreeable to such a move?" he asked St. Denis.

St. Denis thought for a few moments. "I am certain they would welcome the news, Sir. I think it is a splendid idea."

"Then make it so, Louis," Cadillac responded. "I will give you three months to organize the tribe and the men you will need."

LaRouche and his platoon approached the tribal camps alongside the lake. The tribal women saw them coming and began to prepare food for them. They grew tired of the white men coming to demand food and showing up so much more regularly. "We have nothing for them to suspect and we don't need their protection. Why do they keep coming here?" was a common question among the tribes.

LaRouche made himself at home. He walked about the tribe nonchalantly, poking his hand into each kettle to see what was cooking. The other soldiers stood nearby, not wanting to be a part of his carefree actions. The women ignored him and the tribal men looked at him with contempt.

Tooantuh was gathering reeds and firewood for the village fires and was unloading them onto a pile when he noticed LaRouche poking around the village. He grew tired of these intrusions and felt them more and more unnecessary. He frowned with a long sigh as he threw on the last bundle of wood. Then he noticed LaRouche kneeling down next to Ayita, who was stirring the fire under a kettle.

"Good afternoon, there," LaRouche said coyly to her, with a mischievous grin. "Sure would like to get some food for my men. We're all hungry. But for you, I can wait just a little longer." Ayita ignored him, never looking away from the coals. She didn't understand him anyway. She just wished he would go away. Tooantuh grew more agitated and decided he would no longer tolerate this behavior.

"Sure is a pretty day out, isn't it little lady?" LaRouche said sweetly and brushed his hand along Ayita's arm. She stopped stirring the coals and stared down at the ground coldly.

Just then Tooantuh came walking up angrily, shouting in his own language, *"What is this?* What are you doing putting your hands on my wife?" he demanded. "Leave! All of you. Leave! You are not wanted here anymore! You are a disgrace!"

LaRouche was now standing and Tooantuh yelled to his face. LaRouche yelled back at him, "Quiet mister! I've had enough of you. I was just being polite to the lady. She and I were about to take a walk together." He grabbed Ayita's arm and tried to pull her up, but Tooantuh slapped his arm away and then gave him a huge shove, knocking him to the ground. LaRouche had finally pushed him over the edge. Tooantuh pulled his bow and bundle of arrows off of his back and held them in his hand defiantly. The soldiers stood and looked on in shock. Tooantuh stood over LaRouche, gripping his bow and arrows tightly. The soldiers quickly drew their rifles and pointed them at Tooantuh. Tooantuh ignored them. He stood over LaRouche and threw down his bow and arrows in a challenging gesture.

"Stand down, men!" yelled LaRouche from his back. He began to pull himself off the ground. "If he wants to fight me, then he's got it!" He stood eye to eye with Tooantuh and glared at him. Tooantuh turned and walked briskly over to an open area. LaRouche followed directly behind him.

"Sir, don't do this," Sommer begged LaRouche. "We can't be provoking these people, let's just get our things and leave."

"Not me," LaRouche said angrily. "Go if you want to, I'm going to settle this right now!" He began to walk faster towards Tooantuh. He lunged at him with his fist aimed at Tooantuh's back. Just before he landed his punch, another soldier tackled him from behind, startling Tooantuh. Tooantuh turned around in a defensive stance, only to see the soldier pinning LaRouche to the ground.

"I'm not going to let you do this, Lieutenant!" said the soldier. "Now *you* stand down!" The soldier was a newly enlisted man, Thomas Girard.

Girard let him up and LaRouche reluctantly stood and dusted himself off. He glared at Girard, then back at Tooantuh. "You better watch yourself, soldier. There won't be a next time if you try something like that again."

"I'll take my chances, Sir," Girard responded sarcastically. He stared at LaRouche defiantly, his heart pounding in his chest.

LaRouche seemed astonished at his bravery. But, he decided to let it go. "Get your gear," he said coldly. He looked at the rest of his platoon, "All of you. We're getting out of here. Now, let's move out." They marched away as Tooantuh stood and watched them go. Natchitos and Taima stood together, observing all that had taken place.

Chapter 8

Two days later, St. Denis and a small company of soldiers made their way towards Lake Pontchartrain. He was eager to deliver the proposal to Natchitos about returning to the Cane River. The incident at the tribal village had been reported to him, so he left LaRouche at the fort and relieved him of his patrol duties. He thought about his confrontation with LaRouche and wondered how his actions may have affected the relationship with the Nashitosh.

"You're orders were to simply patrol the area, soldier!" he scolded LaRouche. "Nothing more! Your actions could cause severe consequences with our tribal negotiations. You are never to return to that area again. Do you understand? You will be reassigned!"

He sat in the raft and thought more about what had happened. He knew this had not gone over well with LaRouche, but it did not matter. The incident would give the Indians all the more reason to not trust them anymore.

They came to the head of the bayou and pulled their boat ashore. They walked towards the Nashitosh village. As they neared the village, a lot of activity could be seen. The Indians grew anxious as the white men approached. Tooantuh and Natchitos appeared together and approached St. Denis and his men. Natchitos held up his hand to tell them to stop.

"Come no further. We cannot allow you to enter our village," Natchitos said to St. Denis. St. Denis motioned to the soldiers to stay where they were.

"May I approach?" he asked Natchitos. "Not the soldiers, just myself." Natchitos nodded to him. St. Denis walked up to them with a contrite look on his face. "I know what the soldier, LaRouche, has done. I have dealt with him and he will be reprimanded. It will not happen again."

"He is not welcome here anymore," Natchitos spoke in return. "He has dishonored Tooantuh and his wife. Therefore, he has dishonored our tribe."

"I understand and you have my deepest apologies, great chief," St. Denis pleaded with him. "With your permission, I would like to speak to you of another matter." Natchitos looked at Tooantuh, then back at St. Denis.

"What is this matter?" Natchitos asked impatiently.

"I am going to offer Chief Red Hawk the promise of more lands around the lake, including this area," St. Denis said grimly.

"Why would you do such a thing?" Natchitos asked in bewilderment. Tooantuh began to get very angry.

"Wait!" St. Denis interrupted. "I am also here to ask you if you would like to return home!" The expression on Tooantuh's face changed, as well as Natchitos'. St. Denis saw that he had their attention. "Yes, it has been proposed that we return to the Cane River area and re-establish the trading post there as we intended from the beginning, but as your guests. We would only do this if you grant us the permission to do so and allow us into your country once again."

"*Go back, home?*" Natchitos thought to himself. The idea had all but left him now. "It is not my country anymore," Natchitos replied. "The land will be too dry anyway. The land is for the 'great spirit' now."

"But the 'great spirit' holds your spirit there as well, does he not?" St. Denis asked. "The river is there for you as your right. And it always will be. Besides, we have word from our scouts that the land is lush and fertile and waiting to be sewn with the seeds of the Nashitosh once again. If you decide this will be good for you and the tribe, then we shall depart in three month's time."

Natchitos stood for a moment and thought about what he had said. A tear appeared on the side of his eye. He thought for a long moment more, then spoke, "Call to your men, you are welcome to enter our village." They followed Natchitos and Tooantuh into the village. Tooantuh assured the people that it was alright and not to fear the soldiers. Natchitos sat at the head of the fire and asked for the tribal members to come forth.

He spoke loudly and firmly to all of the tribe. "The Lieutenant has proposed to us a wonderful thing. We are to return to our home and let our children grow there." The people smiled with happinesss and relief. The older members hugged one another and laughed with joy.

Natchitos continued, "I have agreed with this man that this will be so, and that we will trade with the white men and let them live among us. This accord will be made so from this day forth."

St. Denis smiled and knew that the beginning of something wonderful was taking place. There was much work to be done yet, but a positive change in the right direction was now at hand.

Natchitos continued to speak to the tribe, "But, before we depart from this sacred land, where the 'great spirit' had led us, we will give thanks to Chief Red Hawk, and the rest of our brothers, with a great feast and dancing at the fire. They have been our hosts and we will honor them with a grand celebration."

The tribe began to make preparations for the feast that was to be held in three month's time. Hunters hunted for wild game, fishermen caught ample fish in the lake and grain was gathered to make bread. Corn was gathered from the crops, as it was the time of harvest. Everyone in the tribe did their part in preparing for the celebration.

Natchitos extended an invitation to the feast to Chief Red Hawk and his tribe. St. Denis delivered the proposal to Red Hawk for his tribe to take control of more lands around the lake and offered a guarded passage for his people to come and go as they pleased to the tribal area of the Houma. Red Hawk was agreeable to everything that was proposed.

At the fort, LaRouche was reduced in rank to Sergeant for his insubordination and was assigned to three weeks of kitchen duty. After cleaning up once again after the soldiers' meal, he stumbled his way back to the barracks. He plopped down on his bunk, next to Sommer, who was writing in his journal. "I can't believe I'm stuck doing kitchen detail. It's making me sick," he whined.

"You picked a fight with a man defending his wife, you idiot," Sommer said firmly, no longer concerned about LaRouche being his superior. "If you ask me, you're lucky Girard stepped in when he did. That Indian was ready to pounce on you like a panther."

"I should have beaten him down when I had the chance," LaRouche said arrogantly. "He's had it coming for a long time! Trust me, I will get him back. I need to get into that camp again. I know exactly what needs to be done."

Sommer put down his journal, "Forget about it, Henri. You're not going back there. You're banned as it is. Just let it go. Besides, how are you going to return without anyone seeing you?"

"I know those swamps like the back of my hand," he boasted. "I'll get in alright, and I know just when to do it, too." Sommer looked at him as if he were crazy. He kept waiting to hear LaRouche's big plan, but LaRouche knew better. He was keeping that one to himself.

Chapter 9

It was the day before the big feast that was to be held at the Nashitosh tribal fire. The cool air of autumn was setting in along the lake. All the preparations were set and the tribe readied themselves for their eventual departure to their homeland on the Cane River. Spirits were high and smiles were on all faces.

Natchitos found some time to go hunting with his youngest son, Nule, now just over eleven years of age. Nule had learned well the art of hunting small game with hand darts, and was also quite adept at fishing. Today, Natchitos wanted to test Nule's skill with the bow and arrow. They crept slowly through the forest, one step at a time. "Listen to what you hear, son," Natchitos spoke softly. "Listen beyond the wind in the trees. Any sound of a deer can be alerted by the scamper of a rabbit or a call from a bird, even a snap of a twig. Stay low and listen." Nule looked everywhere impatiently.

"We must stay on the downside of the wind, so we are not detected. Let us move this way, slowly." Nule followed his father. Suddenly he froze and Nule gasped in surprise. Natchitos turned and put a finger to his lips, then pointed just ahead to their right. Nule's eyes grew large. No more than thirty feet away was the large rack of a male buck moving around. The deer was quietly eating from the forest floor. Natchitos allowed Nule to proceed towards him as quietly as he could. "You be the guide for the arrow, Nule. Take a deep breath and let your instincts come forth."

Nule took out his bow and arrows and steadied one on the bow. He looked back at his father. He nodded for him to proceed. Natchitos sat low to stay out of sight. Nule slowly crept forward to close the distance between him and the deer. Natchitos admired his stealth as a small grin spread upon his face. The deer continued eating unaware of them. Nule found his place and then readied his weapon. He was now ready to take his shot. He put the deer in his sights and pulled back on the bow. The large buck lifted his head in suspicion. The deer spotted the hunter and jumped as soon as it heard the arrow being released. But it was too late. Nule struck the deer with a direct hit to the lower chest. Then another arrow quickly hit the flailing deer. The buck scrambled and staggered on its feet and disappeared into the thick brush.

"Father, I think I hit him, but he ran away!" Nule said excitedly.

"Yes Nule, you did indeed!" Natchitos said with equal excitement. "Now, you must continue to track him. Quickly now, go and find his trail."

Nule quickly found droplets of blood on the plants and on the ground and followed them through the woods for what seemed like hours to him. At last in the dense brush he spotted the antlers of the large buck. The large buck was lying motionless on the ground. Nule instinctively approached the deer slowly. "Look at his belly," Natchitos said softly. "It is no longer breathing." He knelt down beside Nule, who stood proudly, and he hugged him. "You are now on the path of becoming a warrior. I am very happy to see this. You are the hunter and you have succeeded."

Nule beamed with pride as he looked down at the deer and then back at his father. "Father, are we to go back to our lands now? Tell me more about them, Father."

They sat together on the forest floor. Natchitos looked at his son and said, "You were the last to be born in our lands. And, I am now happy to tell you that you will dwell there once again. One day, you will carry the fire of the Nashitosh. I see the eye of a warrior in you, but I also see the eye of wisdom in you. This is the wisdom of a leader, and it is good to see." He patted Nule on his head. He continued, "Our lands are beautiful and green with fertile soil and many animals to hunt.

72

The river is calm and it is a cool place in the summer months. My wish for you is to watch your sons hunt in the forests of our lands."

They stood and pulled the deer onto a tarp made of tough hide, to drag it out of the thick brush and into a clearing. It was very heavy and difficult to drag out of the forest. It took both of them to pull the weight of the deer. Natchitos laughed while they labored with the deer, "You had to shoot the biggest one, didn't you?"

The day of the big feast arrived. St. Denis, Governor Cadillac, and a few other high ranking officials set out with a small company of soldiers in three rafts down the bayou towards Lake Pontchartrain.

LaRouche slipped out of the fort soon after the men had left for the tribal areas. He walked ahead to the edge of the great river toward the rafts and canoes. He untied a small canoe and crawled in as quietly as he could and paddled his way upriver to the next bayou. He paddled through the murky waters, looking all around to make sure he wasn't being followed. He paddled until he knew he was about a half mile from the lakeside. He pulled the canoe ashore and set out the rest of the way on foot.

St. Denis and the other men soon arrived at the lake on their rafts and walked towards the Nashitosh village. As the sun set, Chief Red Hawk and the Acolapissa chanted as they walked into the village of the Nashitosh. Drummers and yells of celebration could be heard at the fire. Torches were lit all around the village and the women put the final preparations on the feast. All gathered around the huge bonfire that was prepared in the center of the village. Natchitos passed the ceremonial drink over to Chief Red Hawk and they drank together. The feast had begun and the food was abundant. They ate deer, lamb, rabbit, and cow. Bread was passed and fresh

73

water was plentiful all around. The dancers performed near the bonfire to the chants of the women with noise shakers in their hands and to the beat of the tribal drummers.

Meanwhile, under cover of darkness, LaRouche snuck into the unguarded village of the Acolapissa, which was now empty. He knew exactly which hut he sought. He crept slowly towards the center of the camp and approached the hut that belonged to Chief Red Hawk. He walked into the hut and saw, displayed on a small wooden shelf on the far wall, the flintlock pistol that was given to the chief by Natchitos. The leather pouch hung below the pistol, hanging from the handle by the leather strap. He took the pistol and hid it under his vest. He grabbed all the gunpowder and ammunition in the pouch and stuffed it into his vest. He quickly hurried out of the hut and ran out of the village back to the woods. He could see the light of the fires and he could hear the yells of celebration coming from the Nashitosh village. He waited in the woods for the precise moment to arrive.

The celebration continued into the night. St. Denis was pleased to see the two tribes celebrating the end of their time together at the lakeside without any animosity. The festivities were going well, he thought. He ate and drank with all of them. Cadillac was pleased to see everyone celebrating together. He leaned over to St. Denis with a goblet in hand and said, "Cheers to you, Louis, for your success! You have done a fine job uniting these people."

"Thank you, Sir."

"I trust your preparations are complete and you are ready to make your way up the river?" asked Cadillac.

"Yes, we will meet with the tribe the day after tomorrow and set out at first light. Natchitos has assured me the tribe will be ready," St. Denis replied.

As the bonfire faded to small flames and bright embers, the celebrating and dancing also came to a close. The tribesmen bid farewell to one another and one by one, the Acolapissa started to make their way back to their village. There were many people scattered about talking in small groups. Some of the tribal men were playing games of chance with rocks and sticks. Through the smoke of the hot fire, Tooantuh spotted a face that he recognized. The white man seemed to have come from the forest and began to blend in with the crowds of people. The Acolapissa continued to slowly depart for their village and the soldiers were making their way back to the boats on the bayou to return to the fort. But the lone white man remained and seemed to be coming back towards the tribal area. The white man locked eyes with Tooantuh's. Tooantuh recognized the intruder immediately. Tooantuh entered his hut and grabbed his bow and arrows and flung them on his back.

"Where are you going, husband?" asked Ayita. "You're going hunting at this hour? They will be starting a new game soon, they will surely ask for you."

"Wait in here, Ayita. I must attend to something." Tooantuh left her with a puzzled look on her face.

Tooantuh hurried outside the village. The moon was almost full and its light guided his way through the woods. Natchitos looked at him quizzically as he hurried by. Natchitos knew that something must be wrong. He called to Anoki and told him to get his bow. "Wait here with me," he told him.

Tooantuh entered the forest, slowly tracking LaRouche. LaRouche waited patiently, his heart beating fast. He knew Tooantuh had taken the bait and followed him into the marshy forest. He hid behind trees, and lay low to crawl from one to another. Tooantuh walked slowly with an arrow docked at the ready on his bow. He ducked slowly under branches and stepped lightly in the thick brush. It was difficult to see even with the moonlight breaking through the tall trees and thick branches. LaRouche was covered in sweat, knowing a confrontation was imminent. But, a little cat and mouse in the woods, woods he knew so well, was what he had planned for Tooantuh. But Tooantuh also knew these woods. LaRouche crouched down low, and waited near a stream just beside a narrow oak tree.

LaRouche could only hear the sound of the water. It had become eerily quiet in the trees. He looked in all directions, but saw no one. He held the loaded pistol closely to his chest. He looked to his right, then to his left. He stayed near the tree leaning his back against it. He sensed movement just a few paces away to his right. *"There he is,"* he thought. He took a deep breath. Then, whirled around to his left and... A hissing sound ripped through the air. He heard a dull *thump* and he winced in pain as an arrow pierced his upper left arm. He fell to his knees and groaned in agony. He opened his eyes to see the arrow had stuck in his arm and pierced through to the other side. Sweat poured from his face and he spun in all directions trying to locate Tooantuh. He looked at the arrow embedded in his arm and groaned again. He gathered himself and quickly placed his arm to the tree while sitting on the ground. He pressed the point of the arrow up against the tree and held the shaft on the other side. With one quick motion, he snapped the arrow off against the tree. He wailed in pain and fell over to his side. He slowly removed the arrow cleanly from his arm and blood immediately poured from the wound. In agony, he tore off a sleeve from his shirt and tied it around his wound to help stop the bleeding.

He heard a twig snap and sensed Tooantuh had come up from behind. Tooantuh approached him slowly, thinking LaRouche to be gravely injured. LaRouche lay still on the ground. Then, he heard another footstep. He rolled over in an instant, pointed the pistol at a surprised Tooantuh and pulled the trigger. *Bam!* The bullet hit Tooantuh in his upper chest near the left shoulder. Tooantuh was blown backwards, landing on his back. LaRouche pulled himself to his knees and slowly began to stand up. Tooantuh lay motionless on the dark ground.

The shot was heard in both tribal areas and braves came running into the woods to see what had happened. St. Denis ordered the men to turn the rafts around after hearing the shot. He jumped from the raft and he and two other soldiers ran in the direction of the gunshot. A loud commotion could be heard from the Acolapissa village. It had become apparent that the theft of the pistol had been discovered.

Anoki was the first to arrive and saw the soldier easily in the moonlight, standing over Tooantuh. He came running right up to LaRouche. LaRouche spotted young Anoki charging him and pointed the gun and fired. But, only a click was heard. The pistol only held one round. Anoki plowed into LaRouche, tackling him to the ground and knocked the pistol from his hands. LaRouche growled in agony and tried to escape. Anoki grabbed the pistol and pointed it fruitlessly at LaRouche. "Tooantuh! Get up!" he yelled to the lifeless Indian on the ground. "Stay there, white man! Don't move!"

St. Denis heard the shouts in the Nashitosh language. He came running at the same time Natchitos and the other braves arrived at the sight of the shooting. Anoki kept shouting, "Tooantuh, Tooantuh!" Then, he shouted at LaRouche, "You have killed Tooantuh!"

St. Denis barked at the soldiers, "Arrest that man, take him to one of the huts immediately and detain him there!" The soldiers dragged LaRouche to his feet and started to take him away, when suddenly Chief Red Hawk and others from his tribe arrived at the scene.

Red Hawk's eyes fell upon Anoki, standing with the flintlock pistol still in his hands. He became incensed at the sight. *"So!"* he yelled. *"This* is how you honor my people's generosity! What kind of *thievery* is this?" He glared at Natchitos. "There will only be *one* answer for this treachery!"

Shocked, Anoki immediately dropped the pistol at Red Hawk's feet. But Red Hawk left it there. He abruptly turned and led his braves away to their village.

Natchitos ran a few steps toward him, "No! It is not as you see!" But it was too late. Red Hawk angrily left the open area in the woods. Natchitos whirled around with anger in his eyes. *"Whose* work is this?" He made a fiery glare at LaRouche who was being held by two soldiers. Then he looked at St. Denis with heartbroken dismay.

"Great chief! I knew nothing of this man's underhanded deeds!" St. Denis pleaded with Natchitos. "I am arresting him and he will be imprisoned for what he has done. You must believe me that I knew nothing of this!" He barked at the two soldiers holding LaRouche, "Didn't you hear me? Take him back to the village and wait for me there, now!" The soldiers dragged LaRouche away towards the Nashitosh village.

Anoki knelt beside Tooantuh, as did Natchitos. Just then, Ayita came running into the woods screaming. "Where is he?" she yelled with panic. "Tooantuh!" she cried, and fell to her knees beside her husband. Several Indians crowded around Tooantuh. They were careful to not let St. Denis or any of the other white men around him. Anoki noticed something from the corner of his eye, yet Tooantuh still lay with eyes closed and motionless. "Father," he whispered softly to Natchitos.

Ayita sat sobbing uncontrollably. Natchitos touched Ayita on the shoulder, "You must be brave. He must be taken to a proper place for mourning." She looked up at Natchitos. "Take Anoki with you. He can help you." Ayita stopped sobbing and looked at her husband then at Natchitos and Anoki with confusion. "He must be taken to the proper place for mourning," Natchitos said again. She nodded her head in understanding.

Natchitos stood and turned to St. Denis. "There is nothing we can do to change these events. We must prepare now for what awaits us. There is no time to waste. Stand with me, Lieutenant, or go on your way and leave us."

"You have my word, Natchitos, I will stand with you," St. Denis said reassuringly. He turned to Cadillac, "Sir, I am afraid that Red Hawk will retaliate for this. Can we send for help to settle this matter?"

Cadillac answered him, "I'll do what I can, Louis, but we are allies of both tribes. It would be easier if we could explain to Chief Red Hawk what happened. But I'm afraid it may not do any good. I will take some of the men back with me in one of the rafts." He turned quickly and made his way down to the bayou.

After everyone had left the area, Anoki quietly helped Ayita take Tooantuh's body down to the bayou and lifted him into one of the canoes. They set out on the bayou in the cover of darkness.

Chapter 10

In the darkness of the early morning, the shouts of war could be heard from the Acolapissa village. The Nashitosh sat in their huts preparing themselves for battle. They inhaled the sacred smoke of their fires and painted images upon their faces. The warriors hastily met in the largest hut and frantically put together a plan for battle. They knew the Acolapissa would not waste time.

St. Denis immediately found the hut where LaRouche was being held. He stormed into the hut, sweat pouring from his forehead. LaRouche lie on a bunk, his shirt stained with blood. *"Savage!"* St. Denis snarled at LaRouche. "You have no idea what you have done. You are not *fit* to wear this uniform!" LaRouche returned an icy glare with a smirk on his face. "You men, take this vermin back to Fort St. Jean and lock him up and let him rot in there!" With that, he stormed out of the hut and made his way over to the gathering of warriors preparing for battle.

The two guards took LaRouche to the bayou and escorted him to one of the two rafts. With his hands tied, they sat him in the middle of the raft and started paddling down the bayou towards the fort.

St. Denis entered to listen to the warriors hastily plan for an attack. St. Denis sat among them, "I have dispatched men to the fort with the prisoner, but it will take several hours for reinforcements to return."

"We cannot wait," Natchitos said. "If help can come from the fort, then, that is good. But, the battle will not wait. We need you here now."

The two soldiers paddled downstream with LaRouche as their prisoner. The rain began to pour on them. He sat in the middle leaning to one side, with his hands tied behind his back. Rain poured down his face. The men paddled feverishly towards the fort, as they wanted to get him in a cell as quickly as possible.

LaRouche sat quietly. Behind his back he tried to hide his hands as he attempted to unfasten the ropes on his wrists. He freed his right thumb and then his forefinger. That was enough to get a hold on the knot that held him captive. He worked slowly, trying not to arouse suspicion. Then he stopped and sat with his head laying low. He waited for the precise moment. The soldier paddling in the back switched from side to side with his paddle. He moved from the left of the boat to the right side. He took a long stroke in the water. Then, suddenly LaRouche jumped to his feet with his hands free and struck the soldier with his fist, knocking him over the edge. "Hey!" yelled the soldier at front as he turned around. But, it was too late. LaRouche grabbed the paddle and whacked him, sending him into the dark waters of the bayou. He grabbed the two rifles and jumped from the boat and waded ashore from the marsh. He fled as fast as he could towards the Great River.

The first light appeared on the horizon and every warrior in camp was posted outside facing towards the Acolapissa village. All the tribal women and girls sheltered themselves in the huts. St. Denis stood alongside Natchitos, keeping a watchful eye. Suddenly, a war cry was heard from the backside of the village. A thud landed upon the head of a warrior posted on the far side. An Acolapissa warrior, with a black painted face, came charging from the woods and landed another blow to the Nashitosh Indian and knocked him to the ground.

A surprise attack from the woods ensued. The Acolapissa began pouring out of the woods that flanked the side where the Nashitosh had expected them. St. Denis and Natchitos were amazed at how quickly they had maneuvered their way into the woods to the other side of the village before dawn. The

Nashitosh warriors charged the attack. Arrows flew, clubs were thrown, and rifles fired as chaos consumed the area.

Another party of Acolapissa warriors ran out of the woods further down the shore to try and draw warriors from the village so they could fight in the open. The plan worked and many Nashitosh charged after them in the open. It was a mighty battle. Blows were struck and arrows pierced the air. Shots were fired and many men fell to the ground. Natchitos fought hand to hand against his attacker. Then, he shot him down with a quick arrow. St. Denis used his rifle and fired at will, trying to discharge as many rounds as possible but the rifle proved to be difficult in the humid, thick air. He could not keep the powder dry in the heat of the battle.

Rain began to fall on the bloody battleground. Blood flowed from arms, faces, legs and chests. The rain grew even heavier and the blood streaked down the bare skin of the warriors and turned the white uniform shirts of the French a soppy, faded red. The rifles were now useless in the rain. St. Denis fought hand to hand combat as well, punching and kicking his attackers. The battle pushed further and further away from the village and the fighting continued. Soon, the Nashitosh realized they were being drawn away from the village purposely. A yell was heard a few hundred yards away at the village. An Acolapissa warrior emerged with his bow held high and yelling in triumph. Natchitos spotted the warrior from a distance. He wiped the blood and sweat that poured down his face in the pelting rain. *The women! They are drawing us out to take our women!* he thought to himself.

"Lieutenant!" he yelled towards St. Denis. "We must retreat back to the village. We must prepare for the next wave!" St. Denis looked about holding a club he had taken from a fallen warrior. He saw that the enemy was making its way back to their village. Dead warriors lay all around the battlefield from both tribes. Some sat on the ground with terrible wounds. Those not injured helped them to their feet and to safety.

St. Denis ran over to Natchitos. "I fear they have dealt us another blow," Natchitos said looking towards the village. "We must go back now!" St. Denis understood what he meant and began to help the other men back toward the tribal area.

When they finally reached the village, they quickly ran to the huts. They found them all deserted. The women and girls had all been taken away during the battle. They were all gone. "This will not stand!" Natchitos proclaimed. "We will take them back and die if we must in doing so!"

They tended to the wounded and sent braves out to gather the fallen in the battlefield. They acted quickly for they did not know when the next attack would occur. St. Denis sat exhausted, but thought hard to determine a way to return the women to safety. Two hours had passed, but still no reinforcements had arrived from the fort. He got up and found Natchitos. "How many warriors do we have that can still fight?" he asked.

"We number about twenty-seven, including you and me," Natchitos guessed. "We have lost twelve souls to the battle."

St. Denis lowered his head in sadness. He looked up at Natchitos after a few moments and asked, "How many can you spare to go and retrieve the women? You have several canoes pulled ashore on the lake, do you not?" Natchitos nodded. "We can try and beat them at their own game. If they can surprise us from the woods, we can do the same."

Natchitos knew what he was proposing. "We'll post twenty-one warriors throughout the woods. We will go deep into the woods and then emerge, scattered in groups of seven in three different areas outside their village. The other six will take the canoes out on the lake and then come about towards the far side of the village. We must do all this without giving up our positions."

St. Denis nodded in agreement, "We draw them out on one side to fight, while the others come from the lakeside and rescue the women. Create a diversion!" He smiled at the keen plan. It was the only choice they had with the few men that remained. "We must move quickly!"

Natchitos and St. Denis quickly passed the plan along to the remaining warriors and gave them their assignments. They gathered up muskets and fresh gunpowder that were stowed away in Natchitos' hut. The rain had stopped, but a thick fog and mist spread upon the land. Six men took three canoes to the lake and paddled far from shore so as not to be seen. They would make their move when they heard the sound of battle come from the shore.

Natchitos and St. Denis then led the other nineteen warriors far into the forest. It was past the mid-day hour as they slowly made their way through the marshes and swamps. They walked for what seemed like hours, rounding their way back towards the enemy village. They headed north all the way up to an area just outside the village. They moved with stealth to the woods edge. The plan had worked, the village was now in sight and the enemy was still within the grounds. The group separated very quickly into three groups of seven and set about eighty yards between one another. St. Denis and Natchitos were in the middle group. They inched closer to the woods edge as did the others. They awaited the signal to come from Natchitos.

Then, on cue, the sound of rifles fired into the air and shouts of war cries spilled forth from the woods. The startled warriors in the village grabbed their weapons and charged from the tribal area. Arrows started to fly from three directions so the Acolapissa charged at all of them. The Nashitosh cut them down as they charged. But more and more warriors came running from the camp. The three groups closed ranks to form a single wall to make a final stand against the charging Acolapissa. They kept charging, fifty yards away, then forty yards. With only seconds before they reached the Nashitosh, St. Denis yelled out loud, "Way low and fire!" In an instant, all of the Nashitosh crouched down low to the ground to reveal Cadillac and a battalion of French soldiers behind them with rifles pointed forward. They had made it in the nick of time and rendezvoused with St. Denis as they had come forth from the woods. They fired in unison and cut down scores of the charging Acolapissa. "Fire!" he yelled again. Smoke filled the air and many warriors fought to the bitter end.

At the same time, the warriors on the lake entered the Acolapissa village and quickly gathered the women and girls from their tribe and led them away. The Acolapissa women did not stand in their way. The warriors left the three canoes along the shore of the village and made their way back on foot to safety.

The Nashitosh cheered in triumph. The remaining Acolapissa retreated back to their village and yielded in defeat. They were no match for the Nashitosh and the French soldiers. The Nashitosh had lost five more souls in the ensuing charge, but the victory was secured with the aid of the soldiers that had arrived in a timely fashion from the fort.

Chief Red Hawk stumbled back into his village. He was devastated at the loss in the battlefield. He saw that the Nashitosh women were gone, but his tribe's women remained. Some sat on the ground sobbing for the lost souls in the battle.

He wearily approached the lakeshore, his face scarred and bloodied. He proceeded to wash his face in the water when he noticed the three canoes sitting afloat together. They were painted with the markings of the Nashitosh. Then, an object caught his eye, sitting on a tree stump a few paces from the canoes. It was the leather pouch containing the flintlock pistol.

Chapter 11

The Nashitosh tribe was reunited once again after the decisive battle. They collected the bodies of their fallen brothers and prepared them to take them home on the long journey. Natchitos swore they would all find final rest in their native homeland. St. Denis and his soldiers helped them get organized for the journey. He knew it would be wise to depart the area as soon as they could for fear of reprisal. The Acolapissa were defeated, but they still had enough warriors to mount a counter attack.

Natchitos sought St. Denis before he and the soldiers returned to the fort. "You have stood by your word, my friend. My people are grateful to you. You have the fight of a warrior in you, and the heart of a true man."

"As do you, Chief Natchitos," replied St. Denis. "But, we must not delay, I will organize my men at the fort, we will depart at first light tomorrow. We shall meet you at the head of the Great River." With that, he left with the battalion and returned to the fort.

Natchitos had no intention of staying in the tribal area along the lake any longer than needed. The entire tribe set out before nightfall in a line of canoes down the bayou. They would travel just short of the fort and spend the last few hours of night on the side of the bayou shores. They lit a small fire and spoke a few words of remembrance of their fallen brothers. "We will mourn them when the journey is completed. The souls of our departed will find rest in our land." Afterwards, they quickly extinguished the fire and waited until first light. A few warriors kept watch over the tribe throughout the night.

At the first light of day, St. Denis was surprised and filled with admiration to find his friends waiting for him and his troops at the head of the Great River. Twenty-five soldiers and the entire Nashitosh tribe set out upon the river and made their way north.   The journey would take weeks with so many people, plus they traveled against the current in the north heading.   After nearly two weeks, they finally made it to the mouth of the Red River and then headed west. On the fourth day of traveling on the Red River, they stopped at the juncture where it flowed into the Cane River.

At the sight of the Cane, they stopped to rest and setup camp for the night. They would complete the journey the next day. Natchitos lit a fire on the banks of the Cane and spoke to the tribe, "These are the waters of our country. May the 'great spirit' bless them as we enter them and let it guide us to our home. We give thanks for guidance and survival. Let this day be remembered."

The next morning, spirits were high as they made their way down the Cane on the final leg of their journey. The winds blew strong throughout the morning. Natchitos stood high in his canoe at the head of the caravan. They rounded the bend and then a familiar hill came into view. He knew it was the sight of their old home. He raised his spear in triumph to signal the other canoes. The tribe yelled in celebration as they pulled ashore.

The old wooden fort stood along the narrow bayou further down the shore, abandoned and dilapidated. Natchitos was glad to see the familiar lands once again. It was late fall, but the lands were still green and vibrant with life. Much rain had come to the area once again and revitalized the soil. It was just as St. Denis had told him.

As the people continued to unload the canoes and rafts on the shore, Natchitos gazed into the woods and toward the hill that led to their old tribal area. His instincts told him something. He was looking for someone, but he saw nothing. A look of concern washed upon his face. Suddenly, a rifle shot was heard from above. One of the braves was struck in the arm and he fell to the ground in pain.

St. Denis looked to the hill. *"Henri!"* he shouted. It was LaRouche. He had been following them the entire journey up the river after he escaped. He looked rugged and disheveled. "What are you *doing*? Have you gone *mad*?"

LaRouche said nothing, but threw his rifle and retrieved another. The soldiers below scrambled for their weapons as did the Indians. LaRouche aimed his gun again, this time at Natchitos. But, before he could pull the trigger, an arrow hissed through the air and struck him squarely in the chest. He arched his back in agony, then, fell forward to his knees. He looked downriver to find Tooantuh standing on a bluff holding a bow in his hands. Tooantuh stood in triumph. The wound on his shoulder was visible but it has been dressed with a dark bandage. LaRouche's eyes grew wide in disbelief at seeing him before doubling over in agony. He fell to the ground and rolled down the hillside. He was dead.

St. Denis couldn't believe his eyes. "Tooantuh is alive!" he said aloud. Natchitos smiled at Tooantuh and was even more relieved to see Ayita and Anoki appear from the woods behind him. They had made it.

Natchitos knew that Tooantuh was not dead as he lay on the ground after the gunshot. Anoki and his father had noticed Tooantuh still breathing as he lay wounded. The wound was shallow and high upon his chest. Ayita and Anoki removed the bullet that same night, then dressed his wounds, and helped him regain his strength during the long journey back home. Ayita had understood when Natchitos told her to take Anoki with her. She knew that he actually wanted her to take Tooantuh ahead of them back to the Cane River. Natchitos knew that a predator's instincts are to never stop until it knows his adversary is gone. He had suspected this of LaRouche.

St. Denis had some men attend to the wounded brave. The wound was not fatal however, for LaRouche had only nicked him in the arm.

St. Denis approached Natchitos, smiling with his arms folded, and regarded him with admiration for his shrewd foresight. "The proper place to mourn, eh?"

Natchitos smiled and nodded to him, "This is the proper place."

The tribe and the soldiers worked together to rebuild the old huts and establish new ones in the tribal village. They worked throughout the winter and into the coming year rebuilding the old fort and expanded the structure for greater usage. The promise of trade would soon flourish as soldiers and other peoples had already begun traveling through the area. The tribe lived in their native land where they had originally settled.

By late winter, the first signs of spring had begun to show in the fields and in the trees. The fort was completed and St. Denis gathered his people and the tribe together to mark the completion of their trading post.

"Let it be known that from this day forth, this fort will serve as our home and trading post among the Nashitosh," St. Denis proclaimed. The land became known to all explorers and traders as the Land of the Nashitosh. The settlement would soon be marked on all French maps, and was called Natchitoches.

One early morning, St. Denis took a long walk along the Cane. He arrived at the hill overlooking the river and saw Natchitos sitting quietly atop the peak. He hesitated for a moment. But, decided to climb up the hill.

He stopped when he reached the top and saw Natchitos staring out towards the rising sun. "Mind if I sit with you, my old friend?" he asked Natchitos.

Natchitos sat for a moment still looking toward the east. At first, St. Denis thought he'd made a mistake by going up there. Then, Natchitos broke his silence. "I was wondering when someone would come and join me up here," he acceded.

He turned and smiled upward at St. Denis. St. Denis sat next to him to share the view. Natchitos fixed his gaze forward once again and said, "Looks like you are the first."

They sat staring at the vastness and beauty of the land before them. Natchitos then spoke to St. Denis, "Our journeys have brought us far. We have seen many things, you and I."

"Yes, this is true. I will never forget them," St. Denis replied. "My happiness is drawn from seeing you and your people in your native homeland. To me, this is the best thing to see."

Natchitos nodded in acknowledgement. "The sign of the true man is when he has chosen the path that has been set before him. This is what I see in you, my friend, and it is good to see."

They sat for a while longer until the sun had fully risen. Then, they both stood and started to head down the hill. Natchitos patted St. Denis on the back and said, "Very brave of you to come up here." They both laughed as they walked down to begin the new day.

Epilogue

That same year of 1714, trade would begin to flourish in the settlement of Natchitoches. Traders would come from all over to trade livestock, pelts, poultry, salt, and other dry goods at the fort. Nearly a century later, it would play a pivotal role as a center of activity in what would be called the Louisiana Purchase. To this day, Natchitoches is recognized as the oldest settlement in the Louisiana Purchase.

Natchitos remained friendly with his brother, Nakahodot. After Nakahodot had traveled for three days towards the setting sun, he and his tribe settled in an area in East Texas near a narrow bayou called Lanana Creek. In 1716, a Spanish mission, called Nuestra Senora de Guadalupe, was established alongside the tribe. The village would become known as Nacogdoches, the oldest settlement in Texas. The tribes established a trade route between the two communities of Nacogdoches and Natchitoches. The road became a well traveled route, and would soon become the eastern part of the trail called the El Camino Real.

St. Denis continued his exploration throughout Louisiana, Texas and Mexico. He made many stops at outposts along the Rio Grande River. Later in 1714, he was charged with violating the Spanish trade restrictions and was imprisoned for a short time at San Juan Bautista outpost. While in prison, he met and fell in love with the commander of the outpost's granddaughter, Manuela Sanchez.

Later that year, Sieur Charles Claude Dutisné arrived in Natchitoches with another garrison of troops and built a larger outpost around the two huts built by St. Denis. The fort was named Fort St. Jean-Baptiste de Natchitoches, in honor of their fellow explorer and former governor that accompanied St. Denis on his first expedition to Natchitoches. The fort was situated alongside a bayou which would be named Amulet.

Meanwhile, St. Denis was ordered to go to Mexico City to defend his actions in the Spanish court. He succeeded in securing his release and thus returned to San Juan Bautista in 1716. He was granted permission to marry Manuela upon his return. He was later named commander of Fort St. Jean-Baptiste de Natchitoches in 1722. He returned to Natchitoches with Manuela and spent the rest of their lives in Natchitoches amongst the tribe and French settlers.

St. Denis died on June 11, 1744. He was survived by his wife and five children. His son, Louis de St. Denis, took command of the fort at the time of his father's death.

The spirit of the Natchitoches Indians lived on into history. It remains an important part of local culture and is still evident today up and down the banks of the Cane River.

About the Author

I would like to thank you for your interest in this little story. As a former resident of Natchitoches, I am happy to be able to share it with you. I know very well the proud and rich history the people of Natchitoches have for their little town. And, proud they should be. Only one settlement can claim it is the oldest in the Louisiana Purchase. This is no small claim either, because anyone who took junior high history, knows just how large the Louisiana Purchase was.

Most residents of Natchitoches all know the tale of how their town was founded, way back in 1714. The legend has been told countless times, of how twin Indian brothers from the Caddo Tribe, traveled in opposite directions from the Sabine River area for three days each. One settled his new tribe in Natchitoches, the other in Nacogdoches, which is in East Texas. Thus explains the equal distance between the two towns from that point, and the approximate location of latitude on a geographical map. Both towns are basically at the same exact point of latitude.

The similarities between the two towns are many. They both have roughly the same population. Both are small college towns and they even have similar downtown areas, including the red brick streets! Another fun fact is the friendly rivalry between the two colleges, Northwestern State and Stephen F. Austin. The last game of their respective football seasons is always between the two universities. The game has been played for over half a century. In 1961, they decided to play the game for a trophy. Northwestern State won the game that year, so the students at Stephen F. Austin decided to carve a 7 foot, 6 inch, wooden statue of Chief Caddo. The statue weighs nearly 300 pounds! They presented it to Northwestern State after its completion. Every year since then, the statue is awarded to be displayed on the victorious school's campus until the following year.

I grew up in Natchitoches from the age of six, until I graduated from college when I was twenty-two. Through the years that I lived in Natchitoches, I gained many friendships and met many people. I have many fond memories of growing up in Natchitoches, too many to share with you here. But, I did see and do a lot while growing up there. I played a lot of tennis on the old courts in East Natchitoches, and spent many a summer day playing golf at the old college golf course (now called Demon Hills) on the Highway 1 bypass. Many of you probably even had me fill your order down at the old McDonald's on the strip (South Drive), back when I was in high school. Speaking of education, I, quite literally, went to school in Natchitoches everywhere! I attended high school at St. Mary's *and* Natchitoches Central. And, I even went to Northwestern State for a little while. I wanted to be an engineer, so I transferred to Louisiana Tech, in Ruston, my sophomore year. Now, I live in Austin, Texas. I try to visit Natchitoches as often as I can, though. My wife and I were able to come and see the 81st Annual Christmas Festival in 2007. It's still the best fireworks around!

I have always wanted to tell the story of Natchitoches' founding. I was always intrigued by the fact that it was the oldest settlement in the Louisiana Purchase, and that the event happened so long ago in American history. The pride Natchitoches has in its history is evident everywhere you go in town. There is a bust, of St. Denis, displayed in the downtown area along Front Street. And, of course, the town is adorned with many fleur-de-lis, the symbol of French influence, all around the town. There are also many street name signs in French.

As early as my teens, I thought it would be a neat idea to re-imagine the story and tell it with a fictional twist with the backdrop of the true and factual events that took place. Every kid (and adult, for that matter) in town knows, and has probably seen, the replica of Fort St. Jean-Baptiste near the campus of Northwestern State. I remember visiting it on a school field trip when I was a youngster. St. Denis' history is well documented, but not much is known about the tribe itself with whom he befriended. So, after doing much research, I was able to gather as much information as possible on the tribe. I then took that information and intertwined as many of the facts into this fictional story. I tried, as best as possible, to retain all the factual events in order to preserve the legacy of the town's founding.

I hope you enjoyed reading *Legend Upon the Cane* as much as I did writing it. It was a fun project to work on and fun for me to imagine living in those early days of the 18th century, writing the story as it happened. Once again, thank you.